Deep Waters

Edited & Designed
by
Whitney Scott

Outrider Press

All characters, situations and settings in this collection are imaginary.

Deep Waters is published by Outrider Press in affiliation with TallGrass Writers Guild

Trademarks and brand names have been printed in initial capital letters

All rights reserved. Printed in the United States of America.
10 9 8 7 6 5 4 3 2 1

Michelle Burke's "Dear One" originally appeared in *Spoon River Poetry Review*, Winter/Spring, 2009

Carol V. Davis' "Marshland" was originally published in *Between Storms (Truman State University Press*, 2012)

"Our Kiss" by Donna Emerson initially appeared in *Carquinez Poetry Review*, 2006

Jane Hoogestraat's "River Roads" was previously published in *Harvesting All Night* (Finishing Line Press, 2009)

"Fried Water" by Lynn Veach Sadler was initially published in *Brother, Can you Spare a War?* (Aquillrelle Press, 2011)

"Crossing the North Sea" by Nancy Scott was originally published in *Schuylkill Valley Journal*, 2009 and in *Detours & Diversions* (Main Street Rag, 2011)

Anthony Russell White's "Early Morning Conversations, Baja" originally appeared in *The Last Known Photograph of Daphne* (Poetry Matrix, 2001) and *Alimentum #2*, 2006

"Remembering Harding Lake" by Nancy Woods initially appeared in *Cirque*, Winter 2009

Paula Yup's "Wilderness" was originally published in *Maine Progressive*, March, 1992

Portions of this book made possible by a grant from Illinois Arts council

Book Design & Production by
Whitney Scott

© 2012, Outrider Press
ISBN: 978-09712903-9-6
Outrider Press
2036 North Winds Drive
Dyer, IN 46311

DEDICATED...

TO ALL WHO SOMEHOW MAKE IT
THROUGH DEEP WATERS

CONTENTS

MARTIN ALTMAN ——————— 11
THE REED

SUSAN BALLER-SHEPARD ——— 12
FLOODING

ELEANOR BERRY ——————— 13
NO OPPOSITE SHORE

DOROTHY BROOKS —————— 14
THE WAY HE WENT

MICHELLE BURKE ——————— 15
NORTH COUNTRY
DEAR ONE

PATTI CAVALIERE ——————— 17
THE ECHO AND THE LAKE

JAIMEE WRISTON COLBERT ——— 21
YOU WILL REMEMBER THIS

DAPHNE CROCKER-WHITE ——— 23
ODE TO ADRIENNE RICH

LEE CUNNINGHAM ——————— 25
MIDNIGHT RUSH TO THE MISSISSIPPI

MARCY DARIN ————————— 31
PERSONAL BELONGINGS

CAROL V. DAVIS ———————— 37
MARSHLAND

ANNE DICARLO ————————— 39
THE POOL

SUE EISENFELD ————————— 45
NORTH RIVER ROUX

DONNA L. EMERSON ——————— 49
OUR KISS

JENNIFER FANDEL ———————— 50
OUR LAST NIGHT

CHARLES FISHMAN ———————— 51
AT THE EDGE

CATHERINE FITZPATRICK ——— 53
SUNSHINE TIME

MAUREEN FLANNERY ———————— 59
DROUGHT

GRETCHEN FLETCHER ———————— 60
DEEP SLEEP

PAT GALLANT ——————————— 61
ONCE AROUND THE LAKE

MARILYN GEHANT ————————— 65
BURIAL AT SEA

WILLIAM GRADY ————————— 67
SUNDAY DINNER

MARY ANN GRZYCH ———————— 71
FETCH

SUSAN HANNUS —————————— 77
THE SEA BEAR

CHARLOTTE HART _____ 80 THE NEW AMSTERDAM	LYLANNE MUSSELMAN _____ 104 ON SEAGULLS
EMILY RUTH HAZEL _____ 81 CROSSING	R.J. NELSON _____ 105 TAKING OUT THE DOCK
NANCY HEGGEM _____ 82 RAGE OF WORDS	VON PITTMAN _____ 107 ROMEO CORPEN
JANE HOOGESTRAAT _____ 83 RIVER ROADS	SUSAN POPE _____ 111 TANGLING with SPRUCE
CHRISTINE LAJEWSKI _____ 84 ASHLEY, NOVEMBER 27, 2005	LYNN VEACH SADLER _____ 115 FRIED WATER
W.F. LANTRY _____ 85 ON POSSIBILITIES	PAUL SALUK _____ 116 DEBAUCHERY
LYN LIFSHIN _____ 86 IN THE VIDEO OF YOUR HEART	GEORGE SAMERJAN _____ 117 HIGH BANK CANTO IV
ELLARAINE LOCKIE _____ 87 THE BATH	NANCY SCOTT _____ 118 CROSSING THE NORTH SEA
SHAHÉ MANKERIAN _____ 88 THE PARIS OF THE MIDDLE EAST	DON SEGAL _____ 119 THREE WORLDS
ALYS MASEK _____ 89 FIRST VALENTINE	GRAZINA SMITH _____ 121 WATER WASHES AWAY ALL SINS
RHONA MCADAM _____ 90 HIGH TIDES	JULIE STUCKEY _____ 126 ALWAYS, ALWAYS THE WATER
KATHLEEN MCELLIGOTT _____ 91 SIREN'S SONG	INGRID SWANBERG _____ 127 FROST MOON
LAUREL MEANS _____ 97 A HOUSE LIKE NONE OTHER	CLAUDIA VAN GERVEN _____ 128 WHAT THE SEA OFFERS UP
KARLA L MERRIFIELD ____ 103 I, SALMON	DIANALEE VELIE _____ 129 AFLOAT IN PARIS

Rebecca Vincent 131
River: A Pilgrimage to Water

J. Weintraub 137
Naples, Florida

Anthony Russell White ___ 138
Early Morning Conversations

Karin Wisiol 139
The Raft at Longs Peak Inn

Marianne Wolf 141
Missing

Nancy Woods 144
Remembering Harding Lake

Paula Yup 145
Wilderness

Peggy Zabicki 146
Lake Michigan

Poetry

1st Place: Shahé Mankerian's "The Paris of the Middle East"

2nd Place: Susan Baller-Shepard's "Flooding"

3rd Place: "Marshland" by Carol V. Davis

Honorable Mention: "The Reed" by Martin Altman

Prose

1st Place: Sue Eisenfeld's "North River Roux"

2nd Place: "You Will Remember This" by Jaimee Wriston Colbert

3rd Place: Rebecca Vincent's "River: A Pilgrimage to Water"

Honorable Mention: "Romeo Corpen" by Von Pittman

THE REED
MARTIN ALTMAN

I ride the reed alone
through the midnight air
to the farthest outpost,
the corner never visited.
Birds mingle with the reeds,
exhaling incantations.
My face cracks against the wind.

I prefer to float between the reeds
and barely breathe their breath
and vanish in the void between them.

Reed follows reed in a tendril march through marsh
and gather at the end to pile, one on one
to build a fortress for those tired of the crowd.

Reed, O common soldier,
don't lose heart.
You can't push back the onslaught of the sea
though you stand guard with thousands day and night.
(It's said a reed will do your will without its breaking.)
Close your eyes and fly with me.

FLOODING
SUSAN BALLER-SHEPARD

Your river in me runs, so deep.
Ardent currents, murky and dark.
When you finally run out of me, I'll weep

like the Mississippi. The dams didn't keep.
You burst over me as though to leave your mark.
Your river in me runs so deep

covering me. What'd you hope to reap?
Dead things float by, so stark,
when you finally run out of me, I'll weep.

Onto my solid ground you'd flow or seep,
making gas lines leak, water on fire, or a power line arc.
Your river in me runs so deep

I'll hold you back. My banks are steep.
Yet you were bound for the coast, I was just a lark.
When you, finally, run out of me, I'll weep.

Your errant waters gouge, they swirl, then creep;
through fertile land, far off lanes, every park.
Your river in me runs so deep
when you finally run out of me I weep.

No Opposite Shore
Eleanor Berry

The lake at evening, calm, shell
pink where the smooth water
reflects the sky. The small waves, a
flickering cobalt script where breezes
crisp the surface, tinged violet
in the cliff-shadow near shore.
Almost happy, I walk the beach, scanning
by habit the storm-tumbled stones
for color and form that draw my eye,
size that would fit my hand, surface
my fingers tingle to stroke.

                              How often, here
and on other beaches, I've given myself over
to this quiet occupation, felt
this near-contentment and melancholy,
this solace, need answered—
need to stand where land stops and look out
on water so wide it seems
to have no opposite shore,
in its tireless shifting of shapes
like all the ways death comes.

THE WAY HE WENT

DOROTHY BROOKS

When the wind whistles like an old lover
my mind roils over something I heard
secondhand years ago: that
he—with his loyal wife in tow—
was luxury-cruising the Greek Isles,
but during their Turkish day trip
on a rickety local bus
careening up the hairpin turns
of the sheer coastal splendor
its driver met a blind curve.

Without warning
the chickens in their slatted cages on top
began squawking, screeching
as the bus veered left, swerved to the right
for the on-coming Porsche. The cliff's edge
crumbled like pie crust—
the bus took rocks, even boulders,
with it: turning, floating down slow-motion,

spitting pebbles like bubbles. Then
the whale splash—the massive crash
echoing wave after wave, circling
all the way to the Aegean shore.
Finally, the blue blanket stillness—
until pure waters smoothed the surface.

Etched in my mind, a last chicken feather
left from the flurry, the scatter—
drifting to the depths like a lost snowflake.

NORTH COUNTRY
MICHELLE BURKE

Fog peels from the lake,
rolling and tumbling over itself
like the undershirt a boy
has cast into the wind, baring
his lean body to the sun
and preparing to dive into water
never so warm it is comfortable.

DEAR ONE
MICHELLE BURKE

The lines on your face grow deeper.
You are more restless each night.
Your dreams are longings for things
that will be imminently lost.

Once, I watched a boy's toy pony
slide over the side of a boat.

There's innocence you can't return to
nor would even if the world allowed.
If there are second chances, they come
as metaphor, horses on the backs of waves.

16

THE ECHO AND THE LAKE
PATTI CAVALIERE

Three photos at the lake that afternoon— in all of them, my eyes are lifeless. My head tilts back and my long blonde hair appears thick from humidity. I am wearing plaid shorts and a sleeveless top; my legs look sturdy and fit. My limp arms are clenching a pair of sunglasses as I look towards the man behind the camera through slit eyes. Even though my relationship with Elvis barely lasted two years, I never forgot a place he shared with me.

His name wasn't really Elvis, it was Eddie. Twelve years ago, we'd met at a dark nightclub in a college town where a jazz band was playing.

"I just drove back from a *gig*," Eddie said. As it turned out, he was a professional guitarist. I didn't have to ask why they called him Elvis, with his black hair and eyelashes, the likes of which might be seen on a doll. He had the tall body of a swimmer and had to stoop to talk to me.

"I just got divorced last month. We have an infant daughter," he said.

I paid more attention to the way he put his lips near my cheek to communicate over the loud music, the serenity setting in his eyes. His aftershave was like fine tea, an exotic scent he'd picked up on a recent trip to an island.

On the night we met, Eddie was wearing a tuxedo, black bowtie, black cowboy boots and carrying his guitar in a black leather case. He carried a guitar around with him like people carry a book, and he'd play that instrument like someone might read a book—waiting for the mechanic to fix his car, sitting on the beach after the sun-bathers have gone home. He brought his guitar the day he brought me to Lake Minnewasaka.

Charmed by his passive manner, the sheen of a five o'clock shadow on his strong jaw, I took up his invitation to follow him on

Saturday nights while he entertained the senior crowd at a local restaurant. Often I'd wear a mini cocktail dress, high heels and stockings. I enjoyed dressing for these occasions—enjoyed being in love.

"I'm with the band," I'd tell patrons when they saw me sitting alone in a corner. They looked forward to seeing me as much as they did hearing Eddie play Cole Porter standards. Saturday night was for watching Eddie perform, for watching other couples dance the foxtrot, for looking forward to our 2A.M. trip to the diner for a bacon-and-egg dinner after his gigs. I loved how easily our lives blended, like flowing water.

―◇――◇――◇―

I thought living with a musician would be like having my own symphony, and that he'd play me songs and write lyrics about our love. So, after only four months, Eddie moved into my house with his six guitars and a modest wardrobe, but endless sheet music, hair products and pills, and a Tupperware assortment of nuts and bolts.

"Eddie, I need to start supper," I said, arms full of groceries with no clean spot to set them down. Remnants of guitar strings or amplifiers were displayed across my kitchen floor, while sitting on my couch were students that he invited into our living room for guitar lessons.

Over time I lost interest in preparing romantic meals; I began to hear his repetitive guitar riffs throughout my day when I wasn't home.

"You have the whole basement for lessons. There's a separate entrance downstairs for strangers," I said. My strained tone betrayed my reasonable suggestion. But if I couldn't make this work with a man who never raised his voice unless he was in front of a microphone—

"The air is too damp in the basement." It wasn't what he said that got under my skin. It was his annoying calm at my frustration with his inconsiderate behavior. The way Eddie eluded conflict reminded me of a river trickling downstream; I became the rock in his path.

"You're not supportive of my career," he told me the month I thought he'd just forgotten to help with the rent. I hated hearing the words that came out of my mouth trying to get him to understand that I felt like his stepping stone to the top of music charts. "I'm sorry that you feel that way," he said. Then he continued to give his students their money's worth—three-hour lessons for $40. After less than one year, I begged him to move out.

Eddie did not move out. That's the summer when he took me to Lake Minnewasaka.

There are five photos of that weekend, but not one of us in which we are together. We stay in a country-like B&B, one with a kind name something like Buttermilk Falls or Whispering Pines. It is painted a faded yellow and has a crooked porch with carved spindle posts, large pane windows, curtains with a tiny print fabric and ruffles. The rooms are small and simple, but clean and fresh as the mug of coffee and blueberry pancakes for breakfast the next day. The place looks as if it should have been a honeymoon. Despite our problems, I want it to be; we even stop by the roadside to snap a photograph on the way to the lake.

Acres of purple salvia are stretched along a flat strip of blacktop with chalk-white lines. I take the first picture of Eddie. He is wearing a straw hat, denim cut-offs and a dress shirt, unbuttoned with the sleeves cuffed to his elbows. The mountains are behind him and the big sky is Crayola blue.

Eddie has his guitar in hand and when I take the second photo of him, shirtless with the guitar case held lengthwise below his waist; he looks as if he isn't wearing anything but the guitar.

He is looking forward to later that night—meeting up with an old friend, a jazz saxophonist who plays a Monday-night gig at a local bar.

"You either love Eddie, or you want to kill him," the friend later tells me.

By now Eddie's love has become a migraine headache. For Eddie, love meant keeping me by his side when he ran his errands to the bank, or when he decided he needed to go to bed at eight o'clock on a summer evening to get up early for a breakfast gig. I am a night owl. My eyes won't stay shut until at least midnight, and my hands and feet won't stay still until then. If only it were because of love that he wanted me to come to bed with him, I would have stayed up all night. For him, it was never love at all. Many years later I begin to receive letters from a woman who does not sign her name. She writes, "he never married me and he'll never marry you unless you have lots of money."

During the afternoon that we spent at the lake, Eddie decides to go for a swim. One bony arm slices into the water, the rest of his body glides along the surface. I ease my shins into the sunny shallow end, stubbing my foot on a stone worn smooth by the constant current. It amazes me how water can do that. I rake my toes into the silt and settle them in the mud.

"Come in the water. You'll get used to the cold," Eddie says, traversing the lake with his long body in slow soothing strokes.

I lean my backside against a warm boulder and stare off in the other direction. I can't recall how I was sorting out the unhappiness that particular day—with him? With me?

But when he swims away, I turn my attention to the lake. It is a lapis blue color, unblemished by a lazy ripple from a rowboat. Surrounding the lake are white granite cliffs that have the appearance of bleached bone, except it is beautifully pitted with flecks of mica and flocked by green foliage and golden moss. Although the park is populated with other visitors scattered throughout acres of wooded trails, we've found this isolated spot in the forest— silent but for the breathing of the trees.

I climb up onto a ledge and sit on the radiant rocks. Eddie snaps my picture. I look sullen, sitting in the shade with a lacy shadow covering my body except for a fringe of sun at my feet. Eddie sits on the ground and cradles his guitar to practice a ballad. At the time, I wanted the lake to be our place. Now, all that matters is that he helped me find it.

"I want to show you something," Eddie tells me. When he climbs up on the ledge beside me, I reach for his hand and stand beside him. We stand at the edge, facing across the quarter-mile of lake below.

"Hello," he calls across the lake. The hollow reply bounces back off the white stone, his words returns as succinct leaden beats of a drum. *Hello, hello.*

An empty quiet follows. I smile like I do when I first meet someone. My heart feels gutted. There is nothing between us but the echo of separate voices. He picks up his guitar to leave. A beach towel tossed like a scarf over his right shoulder, he turns his back and starts to walk to the parking lot. I hang back alone and call into the canyon. My voice is hushed like a whisper, sad but spiritual. I'd finally faced the truth. Why hadn't I been listening to myself?

Although I don't remember what I said that day, I remember how the echo sounded—evocative as a secret.

As often as I thought of returning to Lake Minnewasaka with someone else after I broke up with Eddie, I never did. Sometimes the lake makes me think that it had been a great day. Good thing I have the photos because my echo sounded so perfect.

YOU WILL REMEMBER THIS
JAIMEE WRISTON COLBERT

The day the water sucks out of Kawela Bay is when the old poet confesses his love for you. He tells you you're the beautiful one and you tell him, Oh, you say that to all the girls, and a look at his craggy, saggy, grinning old poet face and you just know this is true. Tell me something I don't know, you say, that I haven't heard before. Meanwhile you see the water receding like there's a giant hand out there dangling from the clouds and reeling it in, like when you were kids and your brother's alive and the two of you holding out your hands, the crystal dark water of the Au Wai settling in, and you're pumping it fast as you can, onto the crabgrass bank in search of crayfish. What did you do with them when you found them? You remember a plastic bucket, your brother's lacy red net like a hooker's stocking, and crayfish the slick auburn color of hair dye scrabbling around in the bucket one on top of the other, looking for the way out.

Your nipples are like pencil erasers, the poet says, and you say OK, that's a first.

But since he's a poet and an old one at that, you'd expect him to make up an elegy of sorts on the spot as more and more of the pale water draws back, revealing a gum line of sand and rock and pastel-colored coral heads, a long stretch of reef then more rock, and the humps of dead fish like they're tiling the sea floor, belly up and shining all silvery in its wake.

Last night when you brought the old poet back to his hotel, he stood on his tiptoes in the elevator and stuck his tongue down your throat, then when the elevator doors sighed open, he marched out in front of you like this was his due, into the waiting arms of his chipmunk-cheeked wife. Perhaps one day he'll write a poem for you, she chirped, winked, then fastening the leash around his neck, black leather with sequins glistening like grains of sand, escorted her husband to their room.

Now though, instead of an elegy the old poet makes a sound like Ohhhhh wrenched out of the hole of his mouth, and he grabs his flabby chest, sinking down on his knees in front of the vast expanse of beach as the water shrinks back and back and back until it's a blink on the horizon, like he's praying to this new waterless world. And you can't not remember it, clutching the koa urn with your brother's ashes against your chest in the back seat of your father's Plymouth, your mother up front and she's asking you who you are with, over and over until you name it, your brother, grit and bone and the dry little chunks of him that later, the funeral done and everyone gone, you would drizzle into this ocean, his name on your tongue unrelenting as a song that keeps replaying, a rerun whose images will never again be new. The taste of this absence, like everything and nothing at all.

ODE TO ADRIENNE RICH
DAPHNE CROCKER-WHITE

I envy Adrienne Rich
diving into that wreck
by choice—
my corpses float to the surface
have angry fish-eaten eyes
flash signs of good fortune
and golden treasure
that lie
like rusty chains and old whiskey bottles
just out of reach
even in my dreams
the water closes in from both sides
high tide and waterfalls on beaches
leave me no room for maneuvering
I drown in either fresh or salt water
until some men take me into a room
and I can't remember the rest of the dream
except for the large flaccid whale
dead on the beach after the bloody eruption
suddenly I know I'll never know
was never supposed to know

24

Midnight Rush to the Mississippi

Lee Cunningham

Greta stepped out of the barn and pushed the heavy Dutch door closed behind her. The sunny afternoon had gone dark. Strange weather for June, she thought. Yesterday—Friday— had been their last day of school for the sixth graders. They had planned a picnic to celebrate their moving into the junior high building for the next three years. Surprise—wet, heavy snow blanketed the world on Friday morning, so the idea of a picnic was such a joke! Branches of flowering trees bent low. Some snapped under the weight of the snow. Snowballs flew in all directions. One group of girls had set up an assembly line of three snowball makers to fuel two snowball throwers. What a treat! They were starting a snowman when they were herded inside. The weather couldn't get any stranger.

As she walked toward the house on Saturday, though, small streaks of lightning flickered in the dark, voluminous cloud bank building in the western sky. Just as she noticed the cloud, a big wet splat slapped the top of her head, then trickled down the back of her neck. Something white jumping up out of the grass ahead of her caught her eye. Hail? Cold rain, pushed by wind, seemed to twine around her. Seconds later, big, heavy drops fell fast and she began to gasp for air. Her thin cotton shirt offered little defense against the hailstones that hit her back as she bent forward to protect her eyes. She bent forward, threw one arm over her head and cupped the other over her nose like an umbrella to keep her from inhaling rain water.

"Hurry up, Greta. Careful. The grass is slippery." Her mom had opened the door to the enclosed back porch. She stood on an old throw rug, put there to catch any barn souvenirs, fresh mowed grass, leaves, sand, gravel, field dirt and wet shoe before they got into her clean house.

Electricity had not yet come to the farm but the Rural Electrification Agency was promising "soon." The washing machine ran on gasoline and required a long hose to carry the exhaust out of the house and a safe distance away.

When Greta shot through the door with the shape and speed of a cannonball, her mom caught her and stopped her right there on the rug! Greta straightened up; she felt as if she had just come up from a high dive into the swimming pool in town. She closed the door behind her, fighting the circling wind.

Mom's familiar hands draped a dry towel over Greta's wet head and blotted the run-off.

"Wow! I have never been in such a rain before. There's no space between the drops! And cold! But the cows are all in the barn and fed, waiting for you and Dad to come out to milk them." Greta was being silly so her mom knew she was all right.

"Here's another dry towel. Get out of those wet clothes and dry yourself off. I'll be right back." Her mother disappeared from the doorway for the moment. When Greta tried to dry her back, she felt some painful areas. She knew the thin cotton shirt had not cushioned the direct hits of hail and she could almost feel the bruises growing.

"I've got another big towel and your bathrobe for you here," her mother announced.

Shaking with cold, Greta dried herself more thoroughly and slipped into the robe. Her mother wrapped her in a soft blanket, put her bunny slippers on her feet, and sat her down in the kitchen with her back toward the stove, still warm from the day's baking. The kerosene lamp had been lighted already and she warmed her hands near it. Normally, the lamp wouldn't be needed until around 8:00 this time of year, coming up to the year's longest day.

After some commotion on the back porch, the kitchen door flew open quickly and there was her father, dry as a bone! He had driven his Model A Ford, converted into a pick-up truck, right up to the house! He wasn't even damp!

"Who's in the blanket?" he teased. "What happened to you?" He laughed and played a silly game of peek-a-boo with her. He had learned that making Greta laugh meant she couldn't stay upset with him. It worked. She was laughing in spite of her shivers. Mom was in the living room, building a fire in the winter heater to take the edge off the chill in the air.

Their evening meal waited on the sideboard: potato salad, Spam, and leftover canned string beans with big slices of homemade bread, fresh from the wood-burning cooking range behind Greta. Mom usually baked all day Saturday to get ready for Sunday company, if anyone came – and for next week when the field work would start. Greta could tell there were cinnamon rolls cooling somewhere nearby.

"You have any trouble getting the cows in the barn?"

"No. They came home by themselves and were anxious to get in for a change!"

"Cows know things. I keep telling you that."

"I believe it now."

She got up and walked in her blanket to the window.

The flat pasture land between road and the house glistened with the help of lightning and the little bit of daylight getting through heavy clouds. Water gushed down the incline to the east, under the cattle chute bridge that President Roosevelt's Civilian Conservation Corps had built over the cows' path to the other side of the road and more of our pastures. Water that couldn't get through the cattle chute backed up, flooding over the road. It was still pouring.

"Hello, is this the Operator at. . ."

"You again?" Eleanor, the local telephone operator fumed at her switchboard in the late hours of a Saturday night.

"I have to tell you—warn people in town that a wall of water is coming toward you at about midnight!"

"Will you stop this? Why don't you girls get some boyfriends and go out on Saturday night like normal people? Please don't call me again. I've had five calls like this tonight and it hasn't rained a drop all day!" Her voice rose, becoming shrill. Stop it right now. Murder! Usually it's boys with 'Do you have Prince Albert in the can? If you do, let him out!' Go find them and you can all leave me alone!" She pulled the plug out of her switchboard. "Uff-da," she muttered, taking small pleasure in the all-purpose Norwegian word of disapproval, disappointment and dismay. The clock struck 11:30. The "wall of water" would be drowning them all at midnight. She opened the door of the telephone office and listened. "Oh, my God!" Men were running across Main Street, gathering up their families. Elmer Johnson's oldest boy ran up the street, stopping in front of buildings to shout, "A flood is coming. Get to higher ground now and don't forget your pet. We've only got a few minutes. This is not a Saturday night joke. Please—leave NOW!"

"Oh, brother! They called Sheriff Mike when I didn't believe them. Uff-da, I'm in Dutch!" Eleanor turned off the Aladdin kerosene lamp, grabbed her pocketbook, took off her shoes, locked the office door behind her and scrammed noiselessly. She jumped into her car and spit gravel as she shifted through the gears, heading up the hill for home.

At the saloon Mike still kept the attention of several old men who had survived WW1, Prohibition, the Great Depression, and now WW2, and were hoping Mike would divvy up the good liquor with his loyal friends "Never gonna happen, gents," Mike muttered. He finally got them out, locked up, and got to work. Mike hurried to move the good stuff up to his living quarters the second floor—the beer, too, if he had time. It was already 11:35. "Damn!"

As soon as he secured his stock, he'd take a bottle of his best scotch, force the car through any water, and get up the hill to visit his never-shrinking Violet Thorssen that night.

Mike knew that sometime tomorrow, mud and stench would rule the world around Main Street for a long time. It would take weeks for the buildings to dry out. Some buildings would have had enough of floods and have to be torn down. The town had survived many floods but the one on its way could be the worst. The farmers would have to go somewhere else on Saturday nights to shop and visit with neighbors and talk weather over a beer or two.

Sad. As the village's unofficial mayor-sheriff, he'd have some thinking and planning to do about rebuilding or relocating; he'd have to re-open his saloon first and gather the men, and any women who wanted to come into "the devil's playground" or "den of iniquity" and plan for the future. He would talk this over with Violet later and get his mind organized.

These men did what was called "exchange work" and helped each other harvest grain, corn, hay and even their precious tobacco. The threshing and silo-filling days of fall saw them gathered around marvelous spreads of home-made food after a long day's sweaty, dirty work. Those were good times. That idea might work well for cleaning up and rebuilding the town, he thought.

Mike liked it there. He had been really busy during Prohibition, running booze between northern Wisconsin where they "grew" Canadian whiskey to sell to tavern keepers or certain booze hounds from Chicago– at a price, any price the traffic would bear. As a wiseacre, he knew people liked him, so he kept them laughing. That had been his best gimmick—next to being the keeper of the bottled pain killers.

As he pulled out of the alley behind the saloon, he made a run up Main Street and around the backs of the stores and houses to check for anyone who hadn't heard the news. Two unrecognizable cars were still there. And Elmer's German Shepherd! When Mike opened the car door, the big dog jumped into the front seat, sat down shivering and whining, and leaned his whole body against Mike, who realized the dog must hear the water coming! "We'll get you home," Mike promised. Dogs know things, he thought.

No one else was on the street. "Okay, Mr. Nazi Dog, let's go." After that, he though, he would drop in on Miss Eleanor.

When church let out on Sunday morning, Greta's father and mother took what looked like the wrong road home, and then she realized they were going to inspect the damage in Cousin Mike's town. It was about fifteen miles southwest of Verona, Dad thought. The water that had come down from the city through our pasture land was moving east, so it had made a 40-mile circuit to get there. The water was still high, still running hard and fast eighteen hours after that first big splat had landed on Greta's head yesterday.

As they approached the bend in the road intersecting with Main Street, Greta jumped up in the back seat and screamed, "Watch out, Dad. The water's right here." He already knew that. The brown water rushed alongside a shelf that had been whittled out of the steep hillside to carry the road they were on. This was the highest floodwater Dad had ever seen here, and he'd grown up in that area, as had Mom. From the road, they looked down on the town which sat on a level with the Kickapoo River Bridge at the other end of Main Street. Both were now under water.

Mike's saloon building still stood in deep water so deep it had touched second floor windows. The rusty brown color visible on the building showed the water level had dropped about a foot already.

People got out of their cars and stood together, watching the floating debris and talking softly. An old ice box floated by, as did gasoline and kerosene cans that had probably stood beside barrels of fuel on a farm. Rationing had not applied to gas for farm work. A tree trunk torpedoed itself at full force into a garage wall and collapsed the entire building, sending up a cloud of dust as it joined the parade of refuse. Several high-pitched screams came up from the crowd when a nude female form floated up near the garage debris. It turned out to be a manikin. An outdoor toilet floated by, among giggles, accompanied by beer and whiskey bottles, a sheet of corrugated tin which supported a chicken passenger that looked totally worn out, tin bathtubs, milk cans and pails, bar stools, lawn chairs, trash cans, rusty barrels used for burning garbage, and even a mattress. Corn on cobs bobbed around. The strangest sight involved two unrecognizable cars that stood front-ends-down in a hole dug by swirling flood water at the corner of Mike's saloon.

Twelve years later, Greta came home for a fall visit. Her mom wanted to go to the fruit farms and buy their usual winter apples, Red Delicious and Greenings. With her mom in the passenger seat of her new-to-her used car, Greta began making her first trip back to the scene of the great flood. Mom gave directions until they got to the place they had parked the morning after the flood when she'd been twelve.

She would not have recognized Main Street. It had become only a short highway through a small park. Only one building—Mike's saloon—still stood. All the others had been cleared out. Basements or foundations had been filled and planted with shrubs and perennials and signs identifying the former occupants. Teamwork under Mike's direction had moved the town to a blasted out, bulldozed, paved plaza on a hillside above flood level. Mike's brick building still sported the high water mark which had been measured and memorialized with "Flood of 1945 High Water Mark." An arrow that pointed to the brownish stain on the off-white bricks declared the eighteen-foot depth of the water that had come through at midnight on a Saturday in early June on its way to the Mississippi. No lives had been lost in that flood, but one person was never seen again— Ms. Eleanor. When asked if he knew what happened, Mike just smiled and shook his head.

Greta remembered the hail and downpour she'd struggled through that Saturday afternoon. She had not only tasted the water that became the flood, she'd even been there for the memorable devastation of that midnight rush to the Mississippi!

PERSONAL BELONGINGS
MARCY DARIN

You see it on your closet floor, peeking out from under a DSW box that contains your favorite strappy sandals. One small tug and the white bag with the snap handle is freed. This will work, you tell yourself. Better than the skimpy supermarket bags that rip under the weight of some scooped kitty litter. Better than your LL Bean canvas bag stained with mushy bananas. It is small, but large enough for a beach towel, a Number 50 sunscreen for *mature* skin, the *Sunday Times* magazine with Mark Zuckerberg on the cover and a twelve-ounce bottle of Vitamin Water you will buy at the 7-Eleven on your way to Fullerton Beach.

"Quit taking *The New York Times* to the beach," your sister warns. "It will scare away men who think you're too smart for them." But you are—smart. You have a degree in history from Columbia University to prove it.

You remember the April afternoon two months ago when you unpacked the plastic bag, staring at the navy blue letters like a gawky ten-year-old taking her first eye test. "Personal Belongings." Then below, "Name" and "Room." In the bottom there is a small fleur de lis design in purple. Classy.

You can't even remember why you swallowed them—the 600-milligram Tylenol prescribed after your surgery for a broken collarbone. You counted out twenty-five, and downed them with two tumblers of Grey Goose vodka you had left over in your freezer from a New Year's party you threw when you moved into your new apartment in Lakeview. You seldom drink that much.

But in the hospital, you drink liquid charcoal, and dribble all over your gown with blue flowers that look like they are sprouting from mud specks. Your sister brings your own stuff—sweatpants with gaping holes where the admitting nurse ripped out the drawstrings, your extra large canary-colored t-shirt with a gigantic sea turtle, a book of Alice Munro stories, your toothbrush, a crossword puzzles magazine, and a pencil that was confiscated by the nurse at the front desk.

In the day room you spend hours teaching UNO to your roommate, a non-verbal Filipino woman who shows you how to do the 'downward-facing dog' yoga position on a flimsy hospital mat retrieved from a day room closet. You hear the muffled sound of slippers shuffling down the newly waxed hallways. You try hard not to shuffle, to walk purposefully in the ballet pink slippers your sister had bought from Target. Wednesday nights, you watch therapeutically approved movies like "Moonstruck" and "Sound of Music" with your silent roommate and others like Rodney who has earned gold stars on his chart. Rodney panicked when he smelled smoke from a birthday cake and pulled the fire alarm clean off the wall of the nursing home he was staying. That's how he landed here. The charge nurse told him if he keeps his nose clean, he can go back soon. Rodney's roommate, an older man in a wheelchair with brown dribble on his whiskers, keeps staring anxiously at the door.

When the movie ends, Zinnia, the charge nurse on duty, yells "Meds," and the bathrobe-clad audience trickles out to the hallway, making a line all way to the nurses' desk.

The next morning, you trudge back to the day room and look out toward Lake Michigan, crystal blue like the aqua velvet shaving lotion your dad used. You tried hard for him, but you were never enough. Not smart enough, quick enough, or pretty enough. Your "Bs" should have been "As." When you were his partner in bridge, you couldn't keep track of trump; your boyfriends were all stupid or potheads. When you got divorced, he just shrugged. "It figures," he said. "You should have tried harder. Your mom and I did."

You look away from the lake, your tired eyes drinking in the pale yellow room filled with long poly resin tables. "I don't belong in here," you inform your nurse. "I want to see my psychiatrist." He is the one with the power, the one who can set you free you, certifying you are no longer a threat to yourself. Or others. Certainly not others. You tell the psychiatrist the same thing you told the emergency room doc. You don't know why you did it. Why does anyone do it?

And then after a few minutes you tell the doctor in the Brooks Brothers suit that you must have been a little down, off your square. You explain about the weeks after your divorce when your daughter moved to New York with her dad and you didn't get out of bed for a week. It was no use; your comforter was crushing your chest like the lead aprons dentists use to protect from radiation.

Genetics, they told you then. The clinic put you on a common antidepressant, one of those new ones with fewer side effects. Except it did have side effects. Big time. Like weight gain. For weeks on end, you scooped out two pints of Rocky Road every night. You did the right things—ten daily laps around the track by your office, the equivalent of one mile, according to the "Ways to a Healthy You" poster in the teachers' lounge. You felt drugged up, a zombie, like someone had wrapped a shawl of filmy muslin over your brain. You couldn't even manage wet eyes when you learned your cousin, the one with twins, was diagnosed with breast cancer. She was thirty years old, for Chrissake. And so you stopped taking the baby blue pills and stuffed the bottle in your underwear drawer under your Spanx. That's when the curtain crashed and you took the Tylenol with the vodka chaser.

A week later, when you finally get out of the hospital, you want to take up your old routine with a vengeance to prove to yourself and to the world you are OK. The next week you are back in the classroom, trying to explain why the Triangle Fire in New York City was so important in labor history.

"It matters," you tell your sophomores. "So many young immigrants died because the doors were locked." You want them to care. Some of them do, and make little tissue flowers and put the names of the victims on a wreath they make out of a wire hanger. But when the semester ends, you are relieved. Now you can breathe a little more easily. Less stress, more time for you. You have always found nature healing. When your marriage was rocky—when you fought every day over who lost the checkbook—you hiked on the gravelly lakefront path, taking comfort in the waves that crashed like broken coke bottles against the boulders.

By now your plastic bag is so stuffed it barely snaps shut. A curled magazine sticks up from under your beach towel with the orange tiger lilies. You decide to walk to Fullerton Beach and wear the strappy sandals. Your shirt with the giant sea turtle covers jean shorts and your "miracle" suit, the purple spandex clutching your abdomen like a Playtex girdle. You walk past the high-rises on Marine Drive, past North Pond where you saw a night heron during an impossibly early Audubon bird walk.

Today there are strollers piloted by tank-topped mothers wearing oversized bling sunglasses. The heat warms your face. Thank God for Vitamin D, the only vitamin lacking in breast milk. You remember how your German pediatrician advised to take Sidney in the stroller so she could get her dose.

Now your blonde, blue-eyed baby girl is in Manhattan, drinking champagne Mojitos and celebrating her twenty-first birthday with her dad and not you. Your relationship has always been fragile. There was something about your chemistry that together didn't jive. You always seemed to try too hard, and she played hard to get. Once, though, in second grade, she had printed a sentence in one of those blue composition books with dotted lines in the middle: "I like it that my mom always smiles when she sees me." Hmm, you smile in your head. That was the year you had to figure out how to strap on her aluminum foil-covered wings in the Christmas pageant. The cardboard wings tilted far to the left, making Sidney look like a drunken angel. Her dad yelled at you, saying you couldn't even fix a kid's stupid wings.

You got a job teaching high school so you could have summers off to be with Sidney. You taught her to make drizzle castles, squeezing globs of wet sand through her little girl hands and watching it plop onto the beach in uneven mounds. You imagined there were sand castles in the sky adorned with gull feathers and mussel shells.

Now you walk alone on the concrete path while bikers whiz by; shirtless men and bronzed women in sports bras, their bare shoulders glistening as they reach for their water bottles. You finally arrive at the beach area, shaped like an old man's crooked finger lying alongside the lake.

You make a visor with your hand and survey the scene before you: a Civil War-like encampment of blue pup tents filled with sleeping toddlers. Slim women lie on their childless abdomens, letting their bikini straps drag on brightly colored beach towels. Humungous coolers on wheels double as card tables and dinettes for entire families.

You pick up an empty bag of flaming hot cheese curls and spread your towel, then strip away your shorts to reveal the lines of blue and green on your thighs that look like a relief map of Iowa, and move gingerly toward the water, stepping carefully to avoid the blue line of zebra mussel shells. Sunscreen has dripped into your eyes, leaving your vision a little blurry. But the lines of heat rising from the sand, like flames from a Gary steel mill, are hard to miss. A few quick steps and you're up to your knees in cool lake water. Best to go in fast. Wading prolongs the anguish.

A lifeguard in a tan helmet rows out thirty feet from shore, keeping some teen-age boys from deeper water. You wade out about ten feet and take the plunge, eyes closed.

You are floating on your back, doing the elementary frog kick when you hear a whistle. Then another. The lifeguard in the rowboat is motioning toward shore. People are scrambling out of the water and going back to their blankets. Then another guard, a woman in a red suit, yells through a bullhorn for everyone to vacate the water immediately. Mothers in dry swimsuits put towels around their dripping kids and make them sit on their laps. Fathers exchange worried looks with eyes narrowed against the mid-afternoon sun and their own anxiety.

The guard has dragged his rowboat onto the sand. You hear a young woman on the blanket next to you tell her friend there is a little boy missing. As if responding to a five-alarm fire, a cavalry of lifeguards converge from beaches up and down the lakeshore. All of them walk into the still water and link arms on the far side of the beach, close to the line of pilings that sit like wooden sentinels. You watch them form a human chain, their feet sinking into the squishy bottom of a great lake carved by glaciers thousands of years ago.

The line of guards moves forward so slowly the water barely ripples. Kids stop making drizzle castles. Laughing teenagers stop throwing Frisbees over the heads of sleeping, bikini-clad girls. Mothers stop whispering to the kids on their laps. And you stop breathing. Everything stops.

Except for the human chain. You see the girl lifeguard on the end, closest to you, the stocky one with a blonde twist on top of her head. She is clenching her fist so tightly you swear you can see the green veins pop on her hands. The boy-man next to her wears a Cubs hat. Their tanned, entwined arms look like pretzels; it is hard to tell where one arm begins and the other ends.

All of a sudden you have memories of Sidney performing at the Ridgeland ice show. The chorus line of twelve-year-old girls linked arms as they danced on choppy ice to music from the Can-Can. The girls' wobbly legs were encased in black tights as they danced and kicked, eventually spiraling out from the center like the paper tongue of a noisemaker.

The human chain has now finished its march across the swimming area, arriving at the small fishing dock about 30 yards away. You watch as an ambulance arrives, its lights flashing scarlet as it reaches the concrete bike path. Another van marked Chicago Fire Department, a sunshine yellow truck, is moving across the sand to the water's edge. Someone from the ambulance takes a bullhorn and tells everyone to leave the beach.

The crowd trickles out, fathers balancing sand-covered like boys on their shoulders. Mothers have made makeshift cabanas of beach towels, wrapping the terry cloth around their girls so they can put on dry clothes without having to walk to the bathrooms so far away.

You linger a few minutes, watching as two of the men from the truck slip on wet suits. And then you, too, join the silent exodus resembling church-goers leaving a stripped altar on Good Friday.

The next morning you pull the soggy green plastic off the Chicago Tribune and hold your breath again as you skim the headlines. There, in the bottom left corner is a short article about Rafael, son of Marcos and Mariel, whose small bloated body was found at 10 pm Sunday night 100 yards off Oak Street Beach. You remember something in Sidney's instructional manual when she took a Red Cross class at the Y. Contrary to what people think, the article said, most victims don't splash wildly, but sink under the water- unnoticed. You imagine Rafael, son of Marcos and Mariel, struggling to keep his quivering eight-year-old lips above the surface of the lake water.

You tiptoe slowly—almost reverently—back to your bedroom to get dressed for your first day teaching summer school, a freshman world history class. Using both hands, you turn the plastic bag with snap handles upside down and watch its contents tumble out: a rolled up tube of sunscreen and a magazine folded back to the crossword puzzle. Bending down, you rescue the bag and toss it back onto your closet floor.

MARSHLAND
Carol V. Davis

We are all intruders here
        though we fool ourselves this late winter day,
carving a place on the banks
            to anchor our heels.
We stretch over the water, hoping
        to slip onto the wings of a Great Blue Heron
but afraid to get caught in the trap of reeds, twisting
            in the foul water.
The marsh ignites: will o'wisps,
sprites, a wisp of flames,
torches held aloft by villagers
        marching on the manor.
We've read too many fairytales
            but this much is true:
I heard voices.
        Not the call of a willet or clapper rail
but a child caught beneath the ceiling of water
            the thin reed of its voice
rising in the brackish light.

38

THE POOL
ANNE DICARLO

Melanie says she dreams of Maui nights, luaus and walks on the beach, dive trips, and volcanoes. Let me be clear—she's not a woman I love, but she is a woman I enjoy. So her fantasy becomes mine. I, too, want those nights, kitschy bars and thick sweet drinks, a room with an ocean view.

I'm a junior associate in a venture capital firm, but Melanie thinks I'm a titan of industry. She thinks I do billion dollar deals. She thinks I bought my used BMW new. She thinks there are no other women.

But there are. With each one, I betray myself. For Luz I become a yogaphile, twisting myself into tighter and tighter concatenations. For Becky I take up poetry, go to readings, and write a haiku. For Jean I become a lover of dachshunds. She'll think I adore that tiny splay-striding canine until we break up. For Melanie I'll learn to dive and float. This trip will be our first and last. I've been watching Paula. She's a runner.

So in three days we'll be in Maui. I'm using points to upgrade our room. Melanie thinks I'm using cash. When you're in this deep, you're in for a pound.

Which explains why I'm wearing swimming trunks and goggles on the Friday before we leave. Which explains why my office thinks I'm on a two-week vacation when the Maui trip is only one week. Which explains the woman across from me—white bikini, dragon tattoo wending across her abdomen, swim cap with plastic flowers perched tight on her head, flat black eyes—Lee, my swim teacher.

Lee works out of a vacant office suite that has a lap pool. It's a silly luxury in this deserted office park, devoid of businesses after the dot-com crash. The pool is heated, and humid clouds fill the room. Lee is emphatic in her demonstrations.

"Hug your knees. Tuck your chin. Hold your breath. Go." My spine points up and breaks the surface. My face is tucked in the water.

I hate the feeling of the water surrounding me, the touch of Lee's hand pushing me down so I can float up. But from the beginning, I've felt that it's Lee who hates me.

"Mis-ter Wentworth," she'd said on Monday as I got out of my car. She was waiting out front, arms crossed, leaning on a faded black convertible. "You've come for lessons?"

"Yes. Hi. Lee?"

She'd nodded slightly, eyes taking in my sedan and khakis, my height, my gym bag.

"Should have worn shorts under pants, Mis-ter Wentworth."

"There's nowhere to change?"

"Change is always possible, Mis-ter Wentworth. That's why you're here, right?"

She'd turned and begun walking away. I followed. She was wearing the white bikini and a white towel tucked around her waist. Over the towel edge I saw an inked aqua scale.

"You are how old?" she'd asked, skimming into the water, rolling onto her back to stare up at a dim skylight, then back over to float over blurred blue tiles.

"I'm thirty-five." I was changing behind a paper screen. I'd found Lee on the Internet. She was the only teacher offering lessons in February. I had to make this work.

"So why now? Why this sudden swimming urge? It's winter!"

I came around the screen. Lee's black eyes darted to my swimming briefs, which suddenly seemed too revealing. "I'm going on vacation."

"I see. A swimming vacation in winter sounds expensive, Mis-ter Wentworth."

"Call me Isaac."

Things got no better in the water. I had expected something maternal, or at least friendly, but Lee was stern.

The water is warm, five feet deep. It should be no problem. I'm over six feet tall.

Lee swims up to me, icy and graceful. "But why? You haven't answered why."

I find her gaze unnerving. It's like she's been around for every lie I've ever told.

I sigh. "It's for a woman," I say. "To keep a woman happy."

Lee somersaults in the water, splashing me as her feet windmill through. I taste chlorine.

"To keep a woman happy?" she says. "So she is happy already?"

Making women happy. My mother, in a purple sundress, trails a hand in the water. She's bought lilies and roses and strewn the blooms in our pool. It's August, twenty-eight years ago, and my father has told me if I don't learn to swim, he's throwing me in today.

I sit in a deck chair, towel around my legs. I'm completely dry. The depths are unknowable, frosted with petals. My mother sings "Summertime." She's urged me in, but the water is so cold. I don't like its silence. We wait for his arrival.

When he comes in it's obvious he's forgotten his promise. He's looking away, face empty like an accident survivor's. He even looks like he's limping.

"Helen, I can't stay," he says.

"Ray?" She hasn't moved her trailing hand, just her eyes.

He shrugs, and I feel his pain, his relief, as he reaches inside his jacket pocket. At first I don't know what it is he is pulling out. He presses the object in his hand, cups it in both palms and tips it into my mother's lap.

She shrieks, leaps to her feet, splashing me as her hand leaves the water.

It's a ponytail, a black pigtail of curls gathered in a scarlet ribbon. A woman has cut her hair and given it to my father.

"Ray!" my mother says. "What is this?"

"We didn't know," he says, "how else to tell you. Abby wanted to start new. She said that now every curl can be mine."

Abby was my mother's friend. I knew by the ribbon what she'd been wearing: a red wrap dress, and red sandals.

My mother's hand flung out. She threw the ponytail in the pool, where it sunk to the bottom.

"You could have told me," she said as my father walked away.

At that moment the water seemed like a thing to me, a wet open mouth. The next day my mother had the pool drained and scoured, and there was no question, as the pool sat empty that summer, whitened and dried like a bone, of either happiness, or swimming.

"I suppose she's happy," I reply now, forgetting who we are talking about, looking around at the narrow lap pool that runs the length of the building; the skylight; the wet tiles, all resting behind a blank conference room door. "What kind of setup is this, anyway?"

Lee looks away, and barks a laugh. She's not smiling.

The pool was a secret, Lee says. Her ex-husband Stanley had converted a conference room, gutted it and tiled it, insulated it so that no one could hear the hum of the jets from outside. He kept the door locked, and held meetings in his own office, or off site.

How the construction had been completed with no one knowing, Lee had no idea. She'd been occupied with gourmet cooking and their teenage son, and she'd whiled away the afternoons caramelizing sugar and searing tuna steaks, while Stanley must have spent the hours swimming laps.

He was venture-capital funded for a startup called Instant Attorney, a company that promised to make a lawyer appear for any customer who required one. Lee thought he was better at making the money disappear.

"He built a pool in a leased building. He hired two attorneys who exhausted themselves zooming anywhere from Redwood City to Milpitas on a moment's notice. He spent the VC dollars and couldn't make payroll. The attorneys quit. I think one sued him for a repetitive steering injury. And as it all crashed down, he stayed here and swam laps like a dictator."

She's swimming on her back and glaring at me as I dog paddle behind her.

Something in the story bothers me beyond her words, but I brush it off.

"On your back," Lee says. "You can't swim if you're not comfortable floating on your back."

I set my arms wide and lean back, letting my feet ease off the tiles. I sink. Of course I sink. How could I not? The water presses on me. My face sinks below the surface, and I panic. The drops are in my mouth. I lose my bearings. I grab onto Lee's wrist, hard, and stand. Her eyes drill into mine, and I know I'm in for a lashing, but my phone rings.

I heave up over the side and splash to my pants.

"Hello?"

"Isaac?" It's Melanie. "Where are you?"

"I'm at McVicker's," I say. "Getting a drink."

Lee stalks past me in the direction of the restroom and opens the conference room door. I'd forgotten it was afternoon; the pool is so dim.

"Oh." She's quiet. I picture that way she has of looking down and rubbing her hand on a thigh, as though she's washing it. "It's kind of early. I just wondered when I should come by tonight."

"I thought we were meeting at the farmers' market tomorrow." She lived across town. It was inexplicable to me how she always found reasons to come over.

"Oh, well OK. If that's what you want."

"OK hon, I'll call you later tonight."

"Right." She's heard it before. I hear her phone click shut.

Lee comes in and shuts the door and it's dark again.

"On your back Mis-ter Wentworth," she says. "On your back."

"So what happened?" I ask, pretending to try a back float but really leaning on the steps. "To make it all crash down?"

It was funny, Lee said, sullen eyes daring me to laugh, that she'd never had an urge to visit the office until that day. She'd been making a pot roast. It was as though she'd heard a siren. She'd lifted her head, set the oven on low, and made her way to Stanley's office.

"The first thing I noticed is that the lot was empty," she said. "And that was a tough trick during the dot com years. All the offices near his were packed. Pizzas were being delivered. A limo honked outside, but as I approached Stanley's side of the building, the far end, all of that dimmed and then winked away. Silence gathered like a wind. Stanley's car was parked out front, next to a burgundy compact with an infant seat in the back. I remember thinking that no child should be carted around like that. And then I went inside."

Suddenly I don't want to hear the rest. I want to swim, but Lee continues.

"Stanley had forgotten to shut the door to the pool. Or maybe he didn't care. No one was there anyway. 'Stanley?' I called, but no one answered. A song was playing, too low for me to hear the words. And I heard water. I followed the sound of water.

"They were in the pool. This pool. I saw exactly where she'd taken off her dress. It was a circle of white silk on the ground. She was dancing in the water. Bending and turning, head down, legs up, then rotating around. She was so graceful."

Lee pauses. The flowers on her swim cap droop.

"Stanley was watching her. He looked so entranced that I doubt anything could have hurt me more. I wanted to cry out, but then I wanted to do something else. I backed out and got in my car." She exhales. "But first I ran my key along that stupid burgundy car and said a prayer for that poor baby."

"And?" I'm unwillingly drawn in.

Lee's black eyes flash, and this time she's smiling. "I made another unannounced visit," she said. "This time to someone who cared."

"Why do you still come here?" I ask.

"Ah, well. I teach now. I've made it my own. No one else would rent the damn place anyway."

As she turns her head and peers up at me, I remember.

Six years ago, I was a new assistant at Tunney Partners. I wasn't quite a secretary, but I was damn close. So when a woman came in during one long afternoon, I greeted her. She was tiny, in a blue dress, black sunglasses masking her doll-sized face.

"Is Scott in?" she'd said. He was one of the partners.

"Yes, but I think he's booked all day," I said, trying to pretend I hadn't personally scheduled all his appointments.

She stood there a moment, then pulled her sunglasses down so I could see the eyeliner pooling in tears around her flat angry eyes. "He'll want to talk to me," she said. "It's about an investment he's funded."

So Scott had come out, and had become interested as the tiny woman hissed up at him in a corner of the lobby. They'd left for an hour in her black convertible. When they'd returned, Scott's eyes were as angry as hers.

"Instant Attorney—shut him down," he'd said to my manager. As he passed by, I'd smelled chlorine. She'd nodded at me as she left, triumphant, and I'd wondered for one crazy moment if they'd just gone swimming.

It was her.

Lee steps out of the pool, watching me as I recognize her.

"I knew you by your height," she says. "I thought you'd remember me, eventually. You saw me on the worst day of my life."

I make a noise.

"Shut up," she says. "Listen. He'd already ruined his dream. It didn't matter."

"You didn't have to do that," I say.

"True," she says. "I didn't. Now I see you here and it's all the same. Lying to a woman. Learning to swim so it's like you always knew how. Why don't you just tell her? Why couldn't he have just told me–'Lee, I want a pool'?"

She'd gotten back into the convertible that day. I remembered because some guys in the office had remarked on it—the beautiful woman, the abrupt hour-long disappearance, the possibility of sighs we couldn't hear, the then-new convertible. Scott had stared us into silence before he went into his office again.

"Bloody infants," he'd said, though he wasn't British, and we'd laughed as the convertible skated away beyond sight.

Two years after that incident, I'd been promoted. Now I'm here for swimming lessons to please Melanie, a woman I met only months ago. I realize that I will not learn to swim today. When it's time to go snorkeling, I'll tell Melanie I have a stomach cramp.

I look back at Lee. She hasn't stopped glaring at me.

"Haven't you ever just needed something that was only for you?" I ask. The dragon lunges as she blows out air. "Yes, you idiot," she says. "That something was Stanley."

She doesn't ask, and I don't tell her, that apart from the memories of the passage of women, the things I keep for myself include: this downward dog; this haiku; this dachshund collar; this quiet, secret pool.

NORTH RIVER ROUX
SUE EISENFELD

Flour. Powdered milk. Butter. A couple cloves of garlic. A hunk of cheese. Pasta shells. After nearly a month of backpacking and rafting in Gates of the Arctic National Park, north of the Arctic Circle in Alaska, that's all my Outward Bound group has left to eat on the last night of the trip. And no one seems to have any idea what to do with it.

We're camped on a sandy bank on the North Fork of the Koyukuk River, our destination after hiking for two weeks from Chimney Lake, where we had been flown in by float-plane, and after another two weeks of rafting the very slow, very low river, which has meant much paddling and less floating and thus very sore biceps and split, bloody fingers.

The jagged, snow-capped peaks of the Brooks Range hug the northwoods forest, already turning to fall colors in late August, and they encircle this river valley, where unseen moose, wolves, grizzly bears, and other large, teeth-bearing mammals sniff us out from afar. Our two-man tents are set up a few feet from one another, near our kitchen mid, halfway between the river and the unexplored boreal forest behind us. It is quite possible that we are the only humans within the 8.4-million acre park.

We've carried seventy pounds on our backs and hiked through trailless tussocks and quarrelsome alders, traversing scree fields thousands of feet high and descending valleys carved by glaciers. We've slept in tents every night, though it never gets dark in the twenty-four-hour summer sun. We've used the shape and movement of the clouds as our weather channel, and we've showered simply by splashing a pot of river water over choice body parts while whistling or singing to ourselves to ward off grizzly bears. And we've cooked our own meals twice a day.

We have, in fact, been living quite large: eggs and hash browns or pancakes with maple syrup for breakfast; for dinner, posole pie baked in a Dutch oven over a campfire, bean thread noodles in Thai peanut sauce, pesto with pasta, and even homemade pizza on our tiny backpacking stove.

But by the last night, we are left with the dregs. My fellow students are three nineteen-year-olds who haven't yet been weaned from mom's kitchen favorites or college dining hall slop. Two of them are on cooking duty this evening.

I'm twenty-five, and after four years of office work in a sterile high-rise where my greatest physical challenge is walking to the water cooler, and after nearly five years with my rugged, adventure-minded woodsman boyfriend Neil, I want to expand my comfort zone, wash off the city-girl patina, and get dirty. I decide to embrace the notion that everything is sweetened by risk, and that the road less traveled can make all the difference. I've come to Alaska to overcome my quarter-century crisis, and to suck the marrow out of life.

I'm wearing chest-high waders, with a light fleece jacket, admiring the river-tumbled stones, veined with white quartz intrusions along the shoreline while the chefs rummage through the white, plastic food-storage barrels looking for something useful. A chorus of "There's nothing here!" and "We're going to starve!" drowns out the lulling trickle of the river. The Outward Bound instructors, closer to my age, drinking coffee while relaxing in their backpacking chairs, throw up their hands and tell the students they're on their own. So I volunteer.

—◇— —◇— —◇—

A year earlier, in Virginia, hovering over the stove in our Sears bungalow in muddy Carhartts and a plaid flannel shirt, Neil whisked together a couple tablespoons of melted butter and flour in a small saucepan, his calloused hands moving gracefully, while I watched. He was showing me how to make a roux.

Neil had already taught me how to "fold" egg whites into waffle batter, how to "cut together" cold butter and oats for apple crisp topping, and how to mince vegetables efficiently with a large kitchen knife. It is Neil who reminded me how many cups make a quart or how you know when whipped cream peaks are stiff enough to stop beating. When the yellow split peas still hadn't softened enough for *dal* after forty-five minutes on the stove, he taught me to cover the pot to pressure the hot water through the legumes. For these questions, I've never called my stepmother, grandmother, or mom.

Neil has also been a recipe inventor, the one who has dreamed up and tested out his own tomatilla salsa, baked mac and cheese with horseradish, and New Mexico-style black beans. For special dinners, he'd grind his own spices with a mortar and pestle to make *garam masala* for Indian dishes or *berbere* for Ethiopian.

His talent in the kitchen is an extension of his try-anything spirit and a naturalist's curiosity, the same personality that has taken him winter backpacking in the Adirondacks, where he's camped in sub-zero temperatures, and bird watching in Big Bend National Park, where he searched patiently in the blazing heat for the rare Colima Warbler.

I give my mother much credit, however; she was an excellent recipe-follower who encouraged my gourmet palate throughout my childhood. After coming home from her full-time work at five-thirty, she'd take a ten-minute nap, and then fix a home-cooked meal for the two of us, using ready ingredients: beef skillet fiesta with canned corn, stewed tomatoes, minute rice, and strips of Steak-Ums; chicken with forty cloves of garlic; chicken with Coca-Cola; or fettuccine with a spinach cream sauce made in a blender — whatever recipes the *Philadelphia Inquirer* printed that week.

Anyone who can read can cook, she demonstrated. Cooking was orderly and safe, like our lives, in our fourth-floor city apartment where I learned to follow directions and not take too many chances. And it was this basic knowledge, plus a couple of Moosewood cookbooks, that got me through senior year of college, when I lived in a house with four roommates who liked to throw dinner parties, and my first several years as a post-graduation, professional adult. I made one-pot meals from recipes with short ingredient lists and not too much fuss.

But thank God for Neil, for I never found myself more on my own than that final evening in the Alaska bush, with no recipe in sight and dinner suddenly depending solely on me.

We've just spent a month surviving in a wilderness few humans will ever explore, learning rope knots, wilderness first aid, route-finding in a trailless terrain, and how to navigate with a map and compass, but dinner is so obvious to me and so hopeless to my fellow group members that I wonder how the three of them will ever make it in the real world.

I direct group member Rob, who had never eaten anything other than his mother's steak-and-potatoes southern cooking before this trip, to boil the pasta and set the pot aside on a flat rock. I busy Josh, a quiet, dreadlocked kid who actually probably has helped his mother in the kitchen, with chopping garlic, with his large, nimble hands. And I assign Jenn, an easygoing but inexperienced college freshman, to be the ingredient-gatherer. Then the four of us, with our scabbed and scraped arms and legs, our unwashed, greasy hair and pungent bodies, crouch around a saucepan as I tell the group to sauté the garlic in butter, tempering the hard-to-adjust controls to prevent it from burning, and then add flour, whisking, until the mixture is slightly browned and crumbly. We stir in the powdered-milk-and-river-water mixture (slightly orange, from the iodine tablets we must use to kill giardia parasites). And as we stir this lumpy, soupy mess—stomachs growling, minds wondering about Plan B—I try to channel Neil's previous encouragement: "It will thicken," he had promised that night in the kitchen. "Just wait."

And it does—a thick-as-the-mud-we-saw-grizzly-bear-tracks-in, white pasty base. Then we slice up our rectangle of hard, yellow, nameless cheese, and stir it in. And when it's as smooth as fondue, we mix the shells and sauce together so that each shell is filled and coated, as any fine restaurant would do, and we serve what was raw and incongruent and impossible into each of our bleach-scrubbed plastic bowls.

And then, on logs, with our sporks, swaddled in the still silence of Alaska, we sit at the edge of everything we once knew about ourselves and everything that has changed, thousands of miles away from home, somewhere in the northernmost mountain range in the world, and we eat.

OUR KISS
DONNA L. EMERSON

I need the kiss I remember: our kiss.
Our kiss right now
feels as deep as the wells on the farm,
one hundred and fifty feet down.
From the minute you turn the pump,
clear, pure water comes up.

When you drink it in, a long drink
without stopping, you know
you've never tasted
water before and you drink it
because it's endless.

When you think you're finished,
the water trickles up the pipe again;
you can hear it, for the next time.

You feel clean, your skin glows,
you feel light filled,
touched between your toes,
to the bottoms of your feet,
your arches even,

and your lips rest, pink,
slaked, without lines.

Our Last Night

Jennifer Fandel

—Ennis, Ireland

There is no river in this town,
the locals said when we inquired.
From the sky to the homes to the ground,

everything was layered in grey and brown.
Our faces, our bodies filled with fire.
We needed a river to navigate the town.

We had one night left to lie down
in each other's arms and kiss everything we admired—
you who were my sky, my home, my ground.

We walked with heavy packs until we found
what turned all men and women liars.
The river made an island of the town.

Our hearts took on water, nearly drowned.
We did not care to walk among the spires
and homes, to breathe in the sky and ground.

Our imminent parting kept us bound.
We walked deeper and deeper into the mire.
Our love was a river hidden in this town.
We searched it—from the sky to the ground.

AT THE EDGE
CHARLES FISHMAN

1. A warm October: goldenrod lights
the dunes, the sky a prism
of lightnings

2. Fishing fleet on the horizon —
gray necklace of fat metal beads —
but what they trawl for, that rich ore
of ocean, is almost gone:
the striped bass my father cast for,
diminished, the sea *harvested*,
robbed of its blood

3. Wind lifts the waves,
a soft lace rustle
Beautiful things tumble
out of those sleeves:
battered twists of drift-
wood, cracked clam shells,
bottle glass ground to green
or purple splendor, this trailing
hem of the sea, an instrument
a thousand miles long

4. What are we here for
if not to know beauty,
to taste the last sweetness
of being, to find the last
scatter of bones?

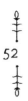
52

Sunshine Time

Catherine Underhill Fitzpatrick

From the day the first crocus popped up until the day the first snowflake drifted down, Missy Henry wailed for her mother.
It was hopeless, all that crying and begging every afternoon. It was the mother who locked the child out.

July 1956

I screwed up my courage and knocked on the Henrys' front door. I wanted to spend a week next door at the Henrys' house about as much as I wanted to get stung by a wasp. But at the beginning of the summer, after I sorta ran away from home and came back again, and after my parents simmered down, Mom and I made a deal. She said if I thought living somewhere else was any better than living with my own family, then I could stay one week with every neighbor on Thistle Way that would have me.

The summer was half over and I'd already stayed with all the good families. The medium ones, too. I was down to the dregs, but I was gol-darned if I'd back out on my end of the deal.

Mrs. Henry glared at me as if I had dropped a bag of poo on her front porch.

"What do you want, Grace?" she said.

Mrs. Henry was still in her housecoat and floppy mules. Her hair was a helmet of swirling pin curls. It was ten o'clock, going by my Cinderella watch.

I explained my deal with Mom and asked if I could stay over. She took a pack of Tareytons from the pocket of her housecoat, shook out a cigarette, and lit it. Streams of gray-white smoke shot out her nose and whisked through the screen door. Some of it got in my throat and I coughed. Mrs. Henry rolled her eyes, like my getting smothered from her Tareyton smoke was a big inconvenience. I hated to think what inconveniences I might accidentally inflict on Mrs. Henry when I was living under her roof.

She opened the screen door a crack and flicked an inch of ash. "I don't care," she said.

I sorta wished she'd said no.

The Henrys had two kids. Missy had just turned six. Her mom had made a marble cake and stuck candles in it and set up a card table on the patio. My sister, Jane, and I were making clover necklaces in our backyard, so we noticed the commotion next door. Missy clunked a table leg and a paper cup filled with Hawaiian Punch tipped over. Mr. Henry let loose with a string of swear words. Missy's Mom told her to blow out the candles so they could eat the damn cake before all her hard work melted onto the plates. It took Missy three tries to blow out all the candles, but she looked so ecstatic I wondered if she'd done it on purpose, to make the happiness last.

Missy was a big-bellied girl with a broad face. Her nose was sort of pushed in, and her ears looked too small. Sometimes her tongue stuck part-way out of her mouth. And her hair was so thin that a little plastic barrette always dangled like a cockeyed earring.

Billy was the only other Henry kid. He was nineteen. Billy worked at a garden center during the day and ushered at a movie theater most nights. He was socking away money to help pay his college tuition. Billy was studying to be a dentist, which I thought was a good thing because his sister's teeth were a mess.

Mr. and Mrs. Henry doted on Billy. I could sorta see why, and my sister shed a little more light on the situation while I packed my suitcase.

"I know something you don't know," Jane said, plopping down on my bed. She was giving me her sly smile, the one that means she knows something I don't know.

"How much?" I knew the drill. Jane and I regarded secrets as moneymaking opportunities. The juicier the secret, the more it was worth.

"Well, let me see," Jane said. "It would have been a nickel, but since you're going to be spending six days at the Henrys', it's a dime."

I shook my piggy bank until a dime dropped from the slot.

"Okay," Jane said, pocketing the coin. "I heard Mom and Dad talking about the Henrys this morning. Mom said she was kind of concerned about you staying there."

I glowed. Mom was worried about me.

Jane went on: "Mom said Mrs. Henry was no spring chicken when she got pregnant with Missy. And Dad said Missy must have been a surprise package."

Jane was talking cuckoo. I wanted my dime back.

I stuffed some clean underpants in my suitcase and thought about Missy. Frankly, I didn't like her much. Listening to Missy bawl her eyes out every day got on my nerves, I'll tell you that.

On Saturday morning I waited until I saw Billy's rattle-trap car back out of the driveway and then I walked over to the Henrys' house. It was starting to drizzle, so I was glad Missy answered the door right away. From the front hall, I saw Mr. Henry slouched in an easy chair in the living room. I said hello, but he didn't seem to hear. I was following Missy up the stairs when I heard glass rattling in the kitchen.

"Mamma's getting Daddy his beers," Missy said. "Daddy likes beer."

At lunchtime Mrs. Henry made us peanut butter sandwiches. She gave Missy and me each a half a nectarine and then delivered more bottles of beer to the living room. I could hear Mr. Henry fiddling with the television knobs, changing the stations.

"Howard, what are you doing?" Mrs. Henry said. She sounded irked.

"Trying to find the damn ball game."

"Sit back down. It'll be on the radio later."

Back in the kitchen, Mrs. Henry switched on a transistor radio. She stood with her back to the sink and leafed through an old *Movie Secrets* magazine. The KMOX weather man sounded excited.

"... straight line winds and hail the size of golf balls are expected to hit Warrensburg and Sedalia hard ... "

I asked Mrs. Henry if Missy and I could go over to my house and play Parcheesi in my room after lunch, though the truth of it is I didn't think Missy was ever gonna finish her gol-darn sandwich. She seemed more interested in poking holes in it. With each new hole, Missy shouted "Polka dot!"

"... numerous reports of trees being down where wind and hail were most intense ... "

"That wouldn't be a good idea," Mrs. Henry said, barely glancing up from the magazine. "It's almost Missy's Sunshine Time."

"... threat exists for severe weather, including wind damage, hail, and isolated tornadoes ... "

Sunshine Time! Was Mrs. Henry taking us to a park? Or to Kiddie Land? I loved the cotton candy at Kiddie Land. Wait. Maybe we were going to go swimming. Things were looking up.

Strong winds and a tornado associated with this storm system caused power outages that affected 700 homes in Topeka overnight."

I was thinking about running home to get my swimming suit. Mom, Dad, and Jane would be on their way to Busch Stadium by now, so the house would be locked. But Dad kept a spare key in a flower pot by the front door.

I was thinking about that key when Mrs. Henry grabbed Missy by the upper arm and dragged her out the back door. I jumped up, too. Were they leaving for the swimming pool without me?

I watched Mrs. Henry half drag, half yank Missy to the far end of the backyard, an area that was completely enclosed by a chain-link fence. Missy kicked and wheeled her legs, but her mother was stronger. Mrs. Henry opened the gate with one hand and pushed Missy into the enclosure. Then she quickly backed out and locked the gate. On her way back to the house, Mrs. Henry rolled her head to one side and then to the other, like Mom does after she's ironed a kabillion of Dad's shirts.

I didn't think Missy's imprisonment was particularly remarkable. I had grown accustomed to the daily spectacle. Everybody had. Missy's wailing was one of the ambient sounds of afternoon on Thistle Way, as reliable as the bells, whistles and chimes that each evening summoned the neighborhood kids home for supper.

Missy had things to do while she was inside that pen. There was a three-step metal slide, a sandbox with plastic bowls and spoons, a beach ball, a Mouseketeer typewriter, a couple of ratty stuffed animals, and a doll stroller. Missy never touched them. She just wailed at the gate and screamed, "Mamma no!"

I'll say this for Missy Henry: the kid had lungs.

I heard a rumble of thunder in the distance. The weather guy was talking about hail and lightning. It was hard to hear him, though, because of all the static.

"The first stroke of lightning can be just as deadly as the last, so if the sky looks threatening, take shelter."

Sunshine Time. Now I got it. That was the Henrys' goody-goody name for the hour or two each day they penned up Missy in the backyard.

Back in the kitchen, Mrs. Henry cut me a look which I took to mean I'd better not start anything. She opened the refrigerator door. Cold air billowed out like fog. She closed her eyes and bent into it. After cracking the handle of an ice tray, she pinched out three cubes and splashed clear liquor from a bottle into the glass.

The radio guy was still talking.

"Lightning can be fascinating, but it is extremely dangerous. It kills an average of sixty-seven people per year in the United States."

The thing was, on the Henry side of the fence Mindy was always so miserable, but on our side everything would be hunky-dory. My sister and I played with our new puppy out there, training him to sit for a bite of salami. We'd run through the sprinkler, string clover-chain necklaces, lie on towels and read library books. In the fall, we'd rake leaves into humongous jumping piles. We'd glance across the fence now and then, and feel a pang of pity. But mostly we wished Missy'd stop wailing.

Mr. Henry was conked out cold. Mrs. Henry had killed off half the bottle and staggered up the stairs. Outside, the sky was greenish gray. Black clouds raced overhead. Tree limbs were thrashing. The wind had tipped over a trash can; bits of newspaper were tangled in bushes. An old sock had slapped against the fence and stayed there.

I was thinking about going out to get that sock when a huge bolt of lightning crackled in the distance. It started to rain hard; angry splats hit the grass and bounced up again. Behind the gate, Missy sank to the ground.

Where the blazes was Mrs. Henry?

"... *a threat of severe thunderstorms over a larger area...*"

I ran through the house and finally figured out Mrs. Henry was in the upstairs bathroom. I smelled bubble bath. She'd taken a record player in there with her. Frank Sinatra was singing "Jeepers Creepers."

"Mrs. Henry!" I shouted. The music was blaring.

"Go away, Grace! This is the one damn time all day I have to myself."

I raced back to the kitchen and out the door. Flashes of lightning were flickering in the clouds. Every few seconds another thunder clap bellowed. I ran to the gate and threaded my fingers through the holes in the wire mesh.

"Missy!" I yelled over the din of the storm. "I'm gonna get you out."

Missy stared at me with white-bulged eyes.

"I'll be right back!" I hollered.

A nasty gust of wind lifted the doll stroller into the air and sent it sailing. "Duck!" I screamed.

Missy was not equipped for speedy response. The stroller clunked her head. With a soft groan, she closed her eyes and then wailed louder.

The key was in the flower pot. I stuck it in the lock and waggled it, but our stupid door wouldn't open. Now it was hailing. Pea-sized bullets bounced around on our front stoop.

I ran to the garage. The door at the back was unlocked. I was in!

The hail pelting the garage roof sounded like a kabillion popcorn makers. I looked for something I could use to get Missy out of that pen. I spotted a stepladder and a small stool, and made a plan.

The hail stopped as abruptly as it had started, but the rain was sheeting down even harder. I dragged the ladder and stool to the section of fence between our yard and Missy's pen. I tossed the stool over the fence, climbed the ladder, and hopped into the pen. My plan worked like a charm.

We were both drenched to the skin. Missy was snotty and crying and trembling, but she still managed to give me one of her goofy smiles. Suddenly, a bolt of lightning struck a tree two houses away. A strip of bark exploded into the air. Missy clung to me as if her life depended on it.

"Shit!" I said. It was the first time I'd said that word. It felt goldarn good, I'll tell you that.

I brought the stool over to the gate and told Missy to stand on it. She was younger than me and lots shorter, but she was built solid as a Buick. Somehow I pushed her over the gate. She landed on soggy ground, and scrambled up again. I flopped over the gate, too. We were free!

I took Missy upstairs. We left a trail of mud, which I didn't care about. Frank Sinatra was still singing.

"Three Coins in a Fountain..."

I got Missy dried her off and found some clean shorts and a top for her. Back in the kitchen, I gave her an Oreo cookie.

I was done staying with the Henrys, I'll tell you that. When Dad gets home, he's gonna beat up Mr. Henry. And Mom's gonna bake a batch of poison brownies and give them to Mrs. Henry and Mrs. Henry will foam at the mouth and flop down and die. Missy won't have to do Sunshine Time any more, either. She's gonna live with us.

The sun was out again. I pried open an Oreo cookie for Missy and turned up the volume on the transistor radio. KMOX was broadcasting the game. Jack Buck was calling plays.

"Top of the first. The stands here at Busch Stadium will be dry in no time. Gilliam leads off for the Dodgers ... High fly ball! One away! Ladies and gentlemen, it's going to be a beautiful day."

DROUGHT

MAUREEN TOLMAN FLANNERY
for Michael Phillips

He died of water,
not much more than a pitcherful.
Run-off on a Colorado highway in July
would have trickled into a grassy borrow pit,
evaporated in minutes.

But it was lingering winter
and melt was made hard again for him
on his ride home that ultimate night.

Unlikely instrument of violence,
a shallow puddle of cold water.

But the sky conspired in this
and the season and the climate
and the improbable specificity of timing
as his front tires hit and skidded
on the small patch of black ice.

Life-water poured out for him
that he might drink deep
from the well of death.

Deep Sleep

Gretchen Fletcher

I dive deep into briny sleep,
a semblance of the salty sea
I swam in before I was washed
onto the shore of life. There, where
time marches on without chronology
things not yet experienced
are forgotten
and things already in existence
can be created.
Submerged, I explore wrecks
lying long-forgotten on the bottom,
now crusted over with a calcified patina.
Just ghost forms of the originals,
they lie oddly juxtaposed
with phylum-less creatures that swim in
and out of hulls and bulkheads.
Their jewel bodies flash past
in the murkiness, and I strain my eyes
in vain to see them again.
Their movements defy Newton's laws;
their forms negate Darwin's theory.
These depths are governed by their own rules.
I hold my breath and buy into the chaotic
order of the place. I'm only passing through,
after all, and will resurface at length.

Once Around the Lake

Pat Gallant

> "What'll we do with ourselves this afternoon? The day after that, and the next thirty years?"
>
> — F. Scott Fitzgerald, *The Great Gatsby*

Maybe it's commonplace in the country, but we New Yorkers have our dreams–moments of abandon, however brief, crack through the traffic, horns and chaos. Grass, trees, birds, lakes–countryside–come to mind. And with these thoughts comes the desire to fulfill the fantasy to find, as quickly as possible, such a scene before the fantasy subsides.

I had one such moment of abandon when my son was nearing his fifth birthday. It was a hot, sunny summer day. We were in our apartment with the air conditioners running to capacity. We were comfortable but it was one of those moments I described when the need to become a part of nature usurped the reason of remaining, what now felt "cooped up" in our apartment. I had other things in mind. F. Scott Fitzgerald and his *Great Gatsby* appeared in my mind's eye. Long, frail white dresses and parasols swam through my head. And water. Boats and water. "The lake," I called to my husband. "Let's go to Central Park, rent a boat and have a picnic by the lake."

My idea didn't seem to have the same draw to my husband as it did to our son, Graig, and to me, but I wasn't about to give up. I finally persuaded my husband and we were off. I gave up the notion of white dress and parasol for the more practical jeans and t-shirt. The Gatsby scene was, after all, my fantasy–one better left unsaid. To expedite things, I brought an empty picnic basket to be filled at the cafeteria by the boat rentals.

The boat man didn't seem to play into my dream. He brought a stark reality to the fact that for him, this was a job, grouchy, and all business. Not to mind! A boat was available. We had purchased our food. We were actually doing this, and rather facilely. The man seemed surprised at my request for life-jackets, responding with a quick "no one ever asks...," but he was fast to get them for us. Perhaps I should have taken as a sign, the dead frog that perched on our boat. It appeared to be alive until the man went to flick it off. It looked as if it had roasted in the sun. Determined, nevertheless, I ignored my feelings of hesitation as we climbed aboard.

Midway across the lake we unpacked our picnic basket. We would eat in the boat, on the water. As we spread out the food for our picnic, a swarm of bees approached. They aggressively went for the food while our son and I sat huddled at the edge of the boat. We decided to try again on land, rowing back to the shore. The bees overwhelmed that area as well; a meal in the park was not to be. Our picnic lunch ended up in the garbage.

After resting for a while on the grass, we walked to our rowboat for our return trip across the lake. When we got to the boat my son said, "No!"

"No what?" we asked.

"No, I won't go," he said, his arms akimbo.

"You want to stay longer?" I inquired.

"No boat!" He shrieked. "I won't go back in the boat!"

"Why dear?" I asked in that sing-song, sweet voice only a mother is all too familiar with, when she's trying desperately to maintain a cool and sees what's coming.

"I won't go, and that's that!" was the answer.

"Are you afraid of the bees? We don't have food now. You don't have to worry."

"It's not the bees. I'm scared," he said, wrinkling his small brow.

"Of what?" my husband joined in.

"Drownding (sic)," was the reply.

"Oh, you won't drown, dear. This water is shallow, see?" And we pointed to the edges where you can see ground under the water.

"No!" was the heightened response this time. He had made up his young mind, his voice rung of determination.

"You're going and that's that!" I demanded.

"No way!"

"Why?" I was panicking.

"It must be deep in the middle or you wouldn't make me wear a life jacket. The boat can tip over, you know."

I was getting nowhere, so tried a new tack: Again, in my syrupy sweet, sing-song voice., I offered, "Oh, what fun Daddy and you and I are going to have. We'll even let you row!"

"Forget it Mommy, it won't work." This from a four-year-old, yet! He's on to my ways already I thought.

"I'm scared and I won't go," he added more vehemently than ever.

"It's no use. I'll row back without him and you walk," my husband said with a sigh.

"Walk? It's all the way around the lake to the boat rental. Graig will never make it. And I can't carry him. He's too big!" My voice was becoming shrill.

"Then you row," my husband answered. "I'll walk back with him."

"I don't know how to row." I was whining now.

"It's simple," he answered.

My husband had his chance and took it. "Anyway, this was your idea. We can't leave the boat here. Maybe Graig can make the walk."

"You know he can't. And I can't carry him across Central Park. We're in the middle of the park—we're not even near an exit!" I said.

"You'll have to try to carry him," was his reply.

"I'll row," was mine.

"I'll meet you where we return the boats," my husband added looking up across the span of the park he would now have to maneuver.

The sun seemed so much hotter. I got in the boat as our son waved victoriously at me. I picked up the oars, held my breath, remembered my husband's words, "It's simple," and began unceremoniously to try and row out to the middle of the lake. I watched as my husband and son walked farther and farther down the path. I managed to get into the middle of the lake – perhaps with the force of my husband's initial "push off" with his foot, but I was beginning to notice I was going nowhere except in circles. Since I was right-handed, that hand rowed stronger than my left, thereby causing me to go in a circle, making no forward progress.

I began to panic. I yelled out to my husband who was already too far into the park to hear clearly what I was saying. He just turned, smiled and waved. After watching me struggle and go in circles, he yelled, "Try going straight. It's easier." He was serious. Good thing he didn't hear my muttering. Did he think I was an idiot? Doesn't he know I know that the shortest distance between two points is a straight line? More muttering from my side as he jogged off with our son. Then tears from me and more than just a touch of panic set in being stuck in the lake – because of how stupid would I feel yelling out to people breezing by effortlessly with their oars!

"Hey, lady," came the voice of a young boy. "Hey, lady, my friend and me. You want we come and row for you?"

Two olive-skinned boys, wide-eyed, eager and mercifully closer to me, waited for my reply.

"I can't get to you," I yelled, panicking.

"We swim out..."

"No! You'll drown." I looked around for their parents and saw no one. Though only about ten-years-old, they appeared to be alone.

"We wade out," they said. Despite my protests, they were on their way, swimming out to me. Their eyes lit up as they pulled themselves up into the boat. After thanking them over and over, I asked if they were with an adult. They said they come to park alone "all the time."

The scrawnier of the two grabbed the oars, headed out to "sea" and with great force, took me for my ride around the lake. His little muscles bulged from his thin but strong arms. The boys were clearly happy to be out on the water and to be my heroes! When we approached the water's edge, they jumped out at the boat rental site, took one glance at the cafeteria, another glance at me, and said, "Boy, we're hungry!" Nothing was too large for this rescue. I reached into my pocket and pulled out a few dollars. They were off in a flash, heading over to buy food, then turned to me.

"Thank you lady. You give us a great day."

The boat man looked startled. "What happened to your husband and son?"

I saw them coming towards us. "They're there," I pointed. "They decided to walk. You know, once around the lake."

Out of the park, back onto the streets, I realize how much I love this noise—how much I love this city. The fantasy subsides, but I am renewed.

BURIAL AT SEA
MARILYN GEHANT

Wounded by armor-piercing blast
USS Arizona rests beneath
harbor waters,
oily residue surfaces, reminds of mausoleum
entombing hundreds of her own.
Layers of silt settle on teak decks
where grasses, orange-pink corals
offer wavy tributes amid
grey oyster and barnacle markers.
No sign of conning tower; aircraft crane
long ago removed for scrap and parts.
In stillness, her twisted metal lies
awaiting death reunions.

National Park divers
swim to the open barbette
of gun turret four, release
sealed urns inside the hull.
Private two-bell ceremonies
flag presentations to family,
rifle salute, reassemble
her full-service complement
one by one.

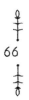
66

Sunday Dinner

William Grady

"Please don't do this."

Billy strains to view his captor, but the rope around his neck extends to the handcuffs holding his arms tightly behind his back. It's not the first time Billy has been in handcuffs. He squints into the setting sun and tries to shake loose. There is an eerie quiet deep in the swamp where even the living creatures lie in silence. Disturbance always draws attention.

"I wouldn't move around much if I was you," comes a warning from the boat floating a few feet away.

Water in the bayou has only two temperatures, bath water in the winter and Earl Grey in the summer. It burns as it laps against Billy's legs.

"You're already startin' to sink. The water is over your knees. If you got a God to pray to, you better get started; some God that turned his back and let you kill them little boys."

"Please. I didn't kill anybody."

"Oh, you killed 'em alright. Jeannie Smith saw what you did to that Stephenson boy, you sick bastard. She was hidin' in the loft. The doc says she'll remember that shit the rest of her life... You did that!...and now Jimmy Wilson."

Billy mouths "No."

"I'm going to remember shacklin' your feet and pushin' you so far down in the Loo-siana mud you'll either sink to the bottom and rot or you'll still be stickin' up pissin' on yourself when the gators come."

Beads of sweat roll down his forehead one drop at a time, stinging Billy's eyes. Blinking makes it worse and he strains to keep both eyes open.

"Most people don't see a gator before it strikes. But if you put a spotlight on 'em in the dusk you see their eyes, bright red, full of fire, just above the water line."

"Please, you've got the wrong guy."

"Look, Billy—we found Jimmy Wilson's feet in your shed. Just his feet! You god-damn animal. We got them feet in the morgue and his mother sits there talkin' to 'em every day. It's the sorriest damn thing I ever seen. You know the voodoos in the Bayou think a corpse without feet can't walk on to the next life, Billy? If you knew what happened to corpses, maybe you would have kept their hands instead of their feet."

"I'm sorry for them, really. Really! But it wasn't me."

"Sorry? I would be too if the hot swamp water was ticklin' my balls. Hey, Billy, you ever see a water moccasin up close before you moved north? Swamp folks call 'em cottonmouths. Sometimes they leave the bank and skim along the top of the water, lookin' like a tree branch about to float by. Then *snap!* They clamp on you with their sharp fangs and don't let go until you're so full of their poison you can't hardly breathe. They say you go blind from the pain for a few seconds, and you try to scream, but your jaws won't work. Then your tongue swells up and sticks right out your mouth. It ain't a pretty sight. Cottonmouths swallow small animals first thing and start digestin' 'em while they're still alive and kickin'. But they can't eat a big man like you all at once. They'll take their time with ya. They'll back away and make wide circles after their first strike, just waitin' for their poison to work. You'll see 'em watchin' ya. When the time is right, they'll open their mouths wide and you'll see the white cotton inside. You don't ever want to see the cotton, Billy. It looks like they're laughin' at you for sure. Then they'll head straight in and start eatin' slow, takin' their time....Sometimes they share with the gar fish, and could be six or eight of 'em eatin' on you at the same time. You ever see the jagged teeth on a gar fish? They use 'em to tear off a good piece of meat, then back up and chew. I guess they'll start with a knee cap, and work their way up. But don't worry, you won't feel a thing. You'll just know they ate your manhood when the water turns all red."

"Please, help me. Please."

"Help you? Can't nobody help you. Soon as your blood hits the water along the bank the gators will come. You'll make a good Sunday dinner for 'em. Did your mama cook Sunday dinner, Billy? Was it good Cajun eatin'? I bet you ate some blackened catfish every Sunday, with fried okra, and hush puppies so full of jalapenos your tongue tingled for a good hour. You know who used to cook a good Sunday dinner, Billy? Jimmy Wilson's momma, that's who. She'd start early, right after church, settin' out a big jug of sun tea. Jimmy'd keep poppin' into her kitchen while she was siftin' her corn meal and ask if the tea was ready. That boy loved his momma's tea. You want to know her secret? She'd throw a pinch of mint in the bottom of the jug. Her gramma taught her that. But she don't make tea no more, Billy. She just sits with Jimmy's feet and talks to 'em like they have ears. She tells 'em stories, and says good-night when she leaves....

She needs to bury her son, Billy. You need to tell me where he is so she can have some peace."

"I can't. I didn't do it. Please help me."

"How's that burnin' water feel around your gut right now? In a few minutes, you'll be tastin' it. Maybe I should put a little mint in your mouth, and the swamp water will taste like Ms. Wilson's tea....Hey, are you cryin', boy? Are you scared? I bet Jimmy was scared, too.... You ever see a gator jump? Most folks think they can't jump 'cause their legs is so small, but I seen one come clear out of the water once and snag one o' them flyin' carps. We got some eleven-foot gators out here that'll snap your head clean off. Your body'll flop around like a catfish jumped off a hook, but your head won't die right away. The last thing you'll hear is the crunch when your skull cracks open and that big gator gulps down your brain."

"Agh-agh!" Billy gasps as he sinks a bit, and struggles to find solid footing.

"Whoo, boy, that was a good one. You dropped a good six inches. I thought you were goin' under for sure. Now it's just me and your head. Just like Ms. Wilson and Jimmy's feet. I'm going to talk to you until your next drop, or till the gators get close. Whichever. Don't matter to me."

"Please. Pull me up and I'll tell you where the boy is."

"Any others with him, Billy?"

"Hurry, please."

"How many others, Billy?"

"There's four boys and a girl. Hurry!"

"We're not missin' any girls. Are you lyin' to me, Billy? I'll push you under right now if you are."

"No, please. It's that Smith girl that's been telling everyone she saw me. I got her yesterday. Please, I think I'm sinking."

"Where are they?"

"Help me up, first."

"Not a chance, Billy. You feel that mud slidin' under your feet? I'd say you got no more than two minutes before this secret dies with you and the gators fight over the lasts scraps of your body. Right now,

I still got time to pull you out. After that, no one will ever know you were here unless a big gator shits out your belt buckle tomorrow."

"Oh, God! They're all in a crypt in the old cemetery. It looks solid, but the top slides off. One man can do it."

"What's the name on the crypt? Hurry up."

"The family name is Foote. Help me up."

"You sick bastard. That's your last name. We should have figured that out sooner. I hope you rot in hell."

"Are you getting me out of here?"

"If I took you in, Billy, the county would have to feed your sorry ass for the next forty years—I prefer swamp justice."

The men stare at each other until Billy's blue eyes slip under the murky swamp water and his last breath bubbles to the surface. Half a dozen tiny bubbles pop silently into the night air, while one circles the spot in defiance before melting away. Twenty feet from shore an eager pair of red eyes dips under the surface.

The boat turns west, heading toward the old cemetery.

FETCH

MARY ANN GRZYCH

A light summer rain started slowly, the kind I love to walk in. It was sunny, a warm breeze barely jostling the leaves. Without a second thought, I put on an old pair of Keds, closed up the cottage and set off down the lane. I'd barely gone a quarter-mile when the first real raindrops fell. I lifted my face to relish each and every one.

My shirt sponged up the water quickly and stuck to me like I was a participant in a wet tee shirt contest. I regretted going out braless and hoped that I wouldn't see anyone I knew.

Walking in the invigorating rain that afternoon brought back memories of similar walks in Chicago, decades ago, when I was a teenager. Mom worked at a small department store near our house. If it started raining near quitting time, I'd walk there, an unopened umbrella tucked under my arm. Frowning, she'd say, "You're going to catch your death of cold," as I handed it to her and turned to leave.

"See you later," I'd reply, not defending myself. Mom didn't understand how being soaking wet could feel good, but she knew that nagging wouldn't change anything. Occasionally, I'd look back through the store window and she'd be standing there shaking her head in silent resignation, probably wondering if her co-workers thought she'd spawned a crazy daughter.

I was so lost in those memories that I didn't hear the car coming until its horn startled me back to awareness. I literally jumped to the side of the road.

"What are you doing out here in this weather?" my neighbor, Bob, asked. A sly smile crossed his face as he noticed the tee shirt clinging to me.

"Just out for a stroll in the rain," I replied, gathering my composure and trying to act casual as I crossed my arms over my wet chest.

He shook his head like Mom had and said, "Flash flood warnings are out. I'm heading back to Chicago before it gets any worse. Jump in. I'll take you back to your place." Until then I hadn't noticed how far I had gone, or that dark clouds were moving quickly toward me, and it was raining much harder.

"I'll be fine," I insisted. "I'll start back now."

Bob hesitated, scowling as he said, "Be careful," and closed the window. An omen of regret gripped my gut as I watched the car's tail lights disappear into a sheet of rain headed my way. I shook off the feeling and turned back toward the cottage. Within minutes the warm summer shower had become a chilling deluge that stung my bare skin like a swarm of angry bees. I prayed that someone else would come along to offer a ride. No one did.

Just a short time ago I had gaily sloshed through puddles, kicking up water like a carefree Gene Kelly singing in the rain. Returning, I trudged through areas reminiscent of Western arroyos that become flash floods with rushing waters sweeping shrubs, debris, cattle, and often people along with them.

The usually quiet creeks that pass under River Road now poured over it on their way to join the Tippacanoe River cascading toward town. Ahead, a scuffed volleyball tumbled across the road rolling over and over. It was chased by cast-off beer cans and a small, limp doll whose wet dress clung to her like my clothes clung to me. Her left arm was missing. Involuntarily I reached across and rubbed my left arm, trembling as a chill washed over me. My stomach churned.

Water was rising in the road with frightening speed. I stopped to look for lights or evidence of life in the cottages around me. I was alone out there, at the mercy of a storm unlike any I'd ever seen. "Oh, Mom, I think I've really done it this time," I whispered, my eyes searching for any sign of a break in the cloud cover that had transformed afternoon into night.

The mud that had been our road, just a short time ago, sucked at my shoes as I forged ahead. I couldn't see the river but could hear objects banging into each other. Another block and the water swirled around my knees. Movement up ahead caught my attention. A cat so soaked his face looked like ET struggled to stay on a tree branch that was speeding toward the river. I grabbed him as the branch went past but he was so frightened that he clawed and bloodied my right arm, then clamped his teeth down on my left wrist as I tried to hold him close. I couldn't calm or control him. He wrenched out of my grasp and was swept back into the current and out of my reach. Afraid that I would be swept away, too, I had no choice but to continue working my way toward the cottage leaving the cat's fate to the river gods.

Branches from a downed tree around a bend blocked the road. They clawed at me, in water now waist high, like the cat had clawed at me. I inched around them carefully then clung to a nearby tree trunk panting for breath. Every muscle in my seventy-nine-year-old body ached. The urge to sit down almost overwhelmed me, but it scared me into action. I continued to fight my way up the road, my legs feeling like there were ten-pound weights on them as I struggled to get air into my burning lungs. When the water got shallower near the cottage, I would have cheered if I had enough breath.

The ground around my place was higher than most of the others that faced the river. An iron breakwater fronted the property, but it was no match for this storm. As the house came into view, the murky river was licking the corners of the foundation. My neighbor's house had water streaming through a broken window and into the crawl space.

Torrential rain continued to pelt me as I climbed the cedar stairs to safety. At the top of the landing I got my first good look at the river roaring past. Visceral fear covered me like a shroud. I stood immobilized by the scene.

Picnic tables, chairs, uprooted trees and propane tanks filled the river like a flotilla heading for town. My pier was gone. I hoped that the cat had snared a ride on a piece of this floating debris. I looked back at my propane tank. The water was pushing against it. It was wobbling. I went back down to inspect the chains and locks securing my boat to its trailer and the trailer to the huge oak behind the house. There was nothing more to do. I shivered uncontrollably, my teeth chattering not only from the unexpected cold, but from the realization that the solitude I'd sought here could be my undoing. Bile rose into my mouth leaving a sour taste as I forced it back down. I'd been so determined to remain independent that I hadn't told anyone I was leaving town. Inside, I tried the phone. No signal.

I washed, tended the angry, red wounds on my arms, gripping the countertop as peroxide stung my flesh, and then dressed in warm clothes.

Wrapped in a blanket to ward off hypothermia, a stash of emergency candles nearby, I settled down in my favorite chair so exhausted that I fell asleep despite the relentless barrage of rain on the roof. I was jolted awake by the sensation of water nipping at my bare feet. The river had moused its way under the doors and into the house. My stomach clenched again and I was tempted to try unchaining the boat. But what would I do then? Become part of a debris flotilla trapped somewhere on the river? No, even alone, I was better off in the house. Patience is not one of my virtues. I needed to let reason reign. I moved what I could off the floor making sure that the bottled water was on the kitchen counter.

The pummeling attack on the roof stopped sometime during the night, but the river continued to rise. Dark silence after the constant pounding of rain was unnerving.

I laid on the couch listening, dreading that the rain might start again.

Water was four inches deep in the house at dawn. By noon it had begun to retreat taking some of the night's terror with it. Outside, uprooted trees lay where my picnic table once stood. A rusty wheelbarrow from somewhere upriver was trapped against them. I had the silly thought that it'd be handy when the repair work began. I tried my cell phone again; still no signal and the battery was weak. My stomach growled and I realized that I hadn't eaten since lunch yesterday. Fortunately, the river hadn't breached the refrigerator door.

Fortified with a ham sandwich and a can of Coke, I swept the muck from the kitchen floor. It was something to do, and lessened the chance of slipping and falling. I heard the whirling of helicopter blades pass upriver but there were no other sounds of life around me. Even the birds were silent.

About two in the afternoon I heard a whining sound. I looked out the windows and saw nothing. "Okay, mind. Quit playing tricks on me," I said to myself. Then I heard it again. Stepping out onto the deck, this time I scanned the water around the house for signs of life. I was about to give up when a dog barked weakly. It was caught in the pile of debris at the river's edge, barely able to hold its head above water. Cautiously I made my way down the steps and over the uprooted trees. A large golden retriever was struggling, his front legs working frantically against the current bent on sweeping him downstream. It had almost claimed him when I grabbed his collar. Wary of being bitten by another terrified animal, I was careful to keep my hands away from the dog's mouth.

"It's okay," I crooned into his ear as I put my wounded arms around him and pulled his shaking body toward me. I stood still for a moment quietly talking. His body continued to quiver, but he finally started dog-paddling, taking some of the weight off my arms. Together we struggled through debris and waist-high water toward the house.

We were almost there when I stepped on something immersed in the murky water—something sharp that cut my right foot, stopping me in my tracks. I could barely step on the foot. I moaned, clutching the dog closer, terrified that he'd get away and I'd slip under the water unable to get up. I leaned my weight on him as he took the lead and pulled me forward. He skittered up the stairs and stood shaking off the river water and barking as I blundered up behind him. Once inside, I grabbed a couple of dish towels drying him as best I could. His tag said his name was Belmont.

"You're okay now, Belmont," I said, scratching behind his ears gently. "I'll bet you're hungry." He wagged his tail and woofed at me as though he understood. I gave him fresh water and the rest of the bread before limping to the bathroom to inspect my foot. A trail of blood marked my path on the wet, beige carpeting.

Washed and dry again, I tended the cut. It was deep, white viscous flesh protruding

It kept oozing even after I cleaned, bridged, and wrapped it. There was nothing more to do but hope it would eventually clot.

Belmont and I spent the rest of the day and night nestled together on the couch in the same intimate way Mom and I cuddled when I was sick or scared. We watched the glacial retreat of the river and the rapid swelling of my foot. By morning I was feverish and becoming addled. My mind swung from euphoria—*"We'll get out of here soon,"* to despair—*"I'll die of infection before anyone finds me."* With a right foot injured so badly, driving when the water receded was probably out of the question.

I slept fitfully until awakened by Belmont. I was so disoriented by then that I didn't know how a dog had gotten into the house with me. "Where'd you come from? What are you barking at? Hush up!" I commanded. In the silence that followed, I thought I heard voices outside, but dismissed them as my feverish mind deceiving me. Then they came again.

"Mom! Are you there?" It couldn't be. I tried to get up from the couch but was too weak to stand.

"I'm here," I shouted, not sure that anyone was really out there. But there was. My son, Al, and grandson, Jay, clad in waders up to their chests, were coming in the door. "How'd you get here?" I asked breathlessly. "How'd you even know I was here?"

"Bob called this morning. He'd seen reports of the river flooding on the news and wondered if you'd gotten home. He said you were walking on River Road, a long way from the cottage, when the rain started and refused a ride back." He paused, looking briefly confused. "I tried calling your phone, but there was no answer. We decided to drive up," Al continued as he bent his lanky, six-foot frame down to remove the waders. "We tried coming straight to the house but

River Road was impassable. We put our waders on and walked from the highway."

"Don't bother taking them off," I said. "As you can see, the river's been inside."

Jay, a mirror image of his dad as a teenager, stayed at the door, wary of Belmont who was sniffing at him, a soft growl rumbling in the back of his throat.

"It's okay, Belmont," I said and the dog returned to my side.

"What happened to you?" Al asked, kneeling in front of me, pointing toward my blood-stained bandage and swollen foot. "Why didn't you tell someone you were coming up here? Where'd the dog come from?"

"It's a long story. I'll tell you on the way home if you can figure out how to get me out of here. I can't walk." Al and Jay fashioned a stretcher out of a blanket, carried me to the car and got me home—with Belmont. Several rounds of antibiotics healed my foot.

That dog rarely left my side while I convalesced. The reassuring sound of his snoring at night made me realize that I don't like living alone after all. I was relieved when I couldn't locate his owner.

Belmont shied away from the river's edge when we returned to the cottage early the following summer, preferring to lie on the deck during the repair work. Then, one mid-summer day I tossed a stick into the river and, to everyone's amazement, Belmont went in after it. He dropped it at my feet, turned and barked. I threw it again—he retrieved it again and "Fetch" became our favorite river game.

THE SEA BEAR
SUSAN HANNUS

My convertible easily maneuvers the curve down to the beach parking lot. The smell of rotting fish fills my nose as I walk, sandals in hand, over pebbles, driftwood and sand. A salty gust of ocean breeze blows my long hair into my face and while trying to push it back behind my ears I notice the carcass of a fur seal rolled in seaweed and sand just a few yards in front of me. The compulsion to see if it is indeed dead overcomes me and I stare at its sunken vacant eyes and rotting mouth. Once it was a living, breathing specimen of its kind with thick fur and puppy-like eyes. I remember reading that its fur had 300,000 hairs per inch. As the waves reach the shore and wash near the seal's body, a wave of sadness for this protected animal washes over me.

I had come to sit on the beach and think. I have decisions to make, and sitting by the ocean has always been a way of distilling my thoughts into decisions. Now I am distracted by the seal's lifeless body. No longer do his eyes have sharp vision or his ears keen hearing. My grandfather told me that the early Europeans described them as sea bears. Seals are sensitive to environmental changes and I wonder if this is why he died.

My husband is leaving me and I think I may die of changes to my environment, too. My world is upended, polluted. I've been swimming around like a sick seal. When I glance over to the poor creature, I want to stroke its smelly fur, acknowledge its death, and witness its final resting place. He was one of thousands that have lost the battle of survival. It occurs to me—will I? My mind gets tangled in this thought, but I shake it off and get up and gather rocks, driftwood, shells and bits of sea glass to scatter over his lifeless body. I find a fallen seagull feather and see it as a gift to wave over the seal's body while chanting his spirit to the other side, as if I had the power to. The ceremony finished, calmness fills me. I sit next to the seal's body adorned with offerings and watch the ocean's waves swirl over my feet. There is comfort in watching the water rhythmically return to its source. A frosted, pitted, bit of cobalt-blue sea glass appears in the sand at my toes like a treasure and I quickly grab it before it can be reclaimed by the Pacific Ocean. It becomes a magical object as I roll it around my fingers and hold it up to the light to witness its glorious deep blue color. Once a piece of trash thrown into the sea, it's now a thing of beauty, having been beaten about by waves, smoothed, polished and tossed up on this beach.

"Cobalt-blue glass is a rare find," says a deep voice behind me. I turn around and see a man about fifty standing behind me. Startled, I don't answer him.

"I comb this beach frequently for glass and I haven't found one yet; you must be very lucky or it's a sign," his says as he kneels in the sand beside me. Then I see him look over to the seal covered in rocks and shells and sea glass and a gull feather stuck into the sand next to it.

"Too many of these lately," he says, shaking his head, "but I have never seen one given a proper burial. Did you do this?"

I want to get up and run, ashamed and embarrassed by what I have done; such a stupid thing for a grown woman to do. But before I can utter a word, he sits down next to me and extends his hand and says, "Hi, my name's Bob Rivers. Wish I had thought to do that myself."

I should feel threated by a strange man sitting beside me, but I don't. Instead I stare out into the ocean enjoying the warm salty breeze through my hair.

"Well, it was nice meeting you," he says getting up and starting to walk away.

I turn and watch his body cast a shadow on the beach. "Wait," I say, having made a decision.

He turns around and walks back toward me and I notice his large, deep-set brown eyes and thick graying dark hair. He's rugged looking as the driftwood, his body lean and his shoulders wide and muscular like a swimmer's. "What can I do for you?" he asks.

"Open your hand," I stand up.

He takes a long appraising look at me, then opens his large tanned hand. I place the cobalt sea glass in its center. "For you."

"Oh, I can't take your sea glass," he says, a look of wonderment on his face as he takes a step backwards.

"A week ago my world broke apart," I tell him, "and I came here to make a decision. You and the seal and the ocean have helped me make one. I'm so grateful—really. Please take it."

Without asking me any questions he closes his hand around the glass and says, "Thank you."

An awkward few seconds of silence passes between us before I look over to the seal's body and think of survival. Sometimes you fail and get washed up on a beach not of your choosing. I still have breath; and for now that is enough and I take one last look at the glistening sea, nod to Bob Rivers, slip on my sandals and head back to my car, walking over dozens of dead fish whose smell no longer bothers me. I turn around for one last look and I see him walking over to the seal's body and placing the cobalt sea glass on top of it.

"Maybe I'll see you around sometime," I call out, the words surprising me as they slip out of my mouth so easily.

He turns and smiles.

THE NEW AMSTERDAM
CHARLOTTE HART

Eyes sky
eyes foam
eyes ocean
chin
eyes to each other
heads
rise
fall
heads in unison with the ship
ocean
sky
ocean
sisters understanding motion

CROSSING

EMILY RUTH HAZEL

We have been to the sandbar
and back—gone to the other side together,
braving the deepwater dip
to get to that oasis in the waves.

The beach at our backs, we have stood
where the waves unleash
all their saved-up energy.
Up to our knees in uncertainty,
toeing the edge, we felt the loose sand
shift beneath our feet
and tried to scramble
up the slope again,
but another wave came
and the water drew back,
weakening our footholds.
The ocean's stronger arm
pulled us into itself.
We had to let go of each other
to swim across the gap
where neither you nor I could touch.
The distance nearly swallowed us.

But then our feet found familiar ground;
we climbed the unstable steps
and walked to the center of a solid plateau,
baby waves breaking around us,
loving our ankles.

RAGE OF WORDS

NANCY HEGGEM

The shower blocks out daily busy sounds,
my mind streams a torrent of words.
Words I would write down,
if it were possible to shampoo,
scrub and scribble at the same time.

Like bubbles down the drain, words
drown when the water is turned off.

My obsession is hearing a phrase
I must make into a poem as soon as possible.
Use pen, pencil, marker or crayon on
notebook, cardboard or Post-it.
Catch that phrase before it flies away
like faces in the window of a speeding train.

RIVER ROADS
JANE HOOGESTRAAT

That afternoon we walked above the river
I wanted you to know everything at once,
a landscape it took me months to learn,
how the light touches a bridge silver
miles away, the streams that lead
into the Missouri below—Hart, Apple Creek—
and the roads that hide along the river,
how one tree in the ravine will turn red soon,
others a paler shade of green to seem
for one fall day as they do in spring,
and the light here, how it is never the same.

How haze hangs over the river roads
even into spring when the fog lifts
quiet laughter in the morning air,
something breaking free, the world for once
coming clean, even then a haze will veil
the currents of the river, lace the road,
and so driving there in early spring
or late summer means following a voice
both soothing and disturbing, although softer
than despair, say as in winter when from rooms
above the city you don't know if people
passing below are speaking or only
following their own white breath.

Ashley, November 27, 2005
Christine Lajewski

You had been perfected
before you came to that midnight shore,
dancing, shimmering like the ancient ivory moon,
casting incandescent ribbons on the dark ripples.
You were gliding forth to gather them
when the black waters closed
over your head and outstretched hand.

You had become so perfect
when you sanctified those waters
with your lost and frozen smile
and your laughter, gently rippling
from the place of your departure.

ON POSSIBILITIES
W.F. LANTRY

> *"I shall unlearn feeling, unlearn my gift"*
> – Trinidadian author Derek Walcott

It is the swirling of currents
around her body that makes me
think of this: O, to be that water,
to be that wind through her hair,
the light glinting unpatterned around her face,
to simply be.

And I find myself fighting against
my own desire to make the vision art,
my own learned wish to sing.
What was handed to me
at some unknown moment over years—
who will take it, now, from my hands?

And she, there, in the small waves of her own making
laughs with a joy I almost know,
turning to me as I watch,
the small drops of water reluctant to leave her skin,
but falling around her in sunlight
falling onto my hands.

IN THE VIDEO OF YOUR HEART
LYN LIFSHIN

the oranges and blues
swirl, waves under
an ocean, a gush of
water, a flash of
blood. It's a tape to
sleep by if I didn't
know it was the
clicks and murmurs
that have to be fixed.
Like a sluice pump,
or the water going
over Otter Falls,
loud enough to
sweep trees up in
its rushing water, the
roots tangling in
the air like arms of
someone drowning
or the pale wrists
of a woman burned
alive, beckoning
or waving goodbye

THE BATH

ELLARAINE LOCKIE

She stares straight ahead
stretched out soaking *au naturel*
in a stark white tub
and trance-like state
Blind to his brush strokes
Pierre Bonnard's wife subject
Portrayed at a time
when water therapy
was treatment for tuberculosis
Or obsessive neurosis
One wonders whether she
wasn't already dead
The water having fatally failed
and the corpse prepared for viewing
with oil-paint preservation
Bonnard's depiction
a conjugal composition inquest
Or whether she has
succumbed to coma
paralyzed by the parade
of people invading her privacy
the Tate gallery
a modern municipal bathroom

THE PARIS OF THE MIDDLE EAST
SHAHÉ MANKERIAN

When you visit Beirut,
stay at L'Hotel St-George
for at least one night.

Request a table
at La Terasse Café
overlooking the Mediterranean.

Ask for Saleem to serve you.
This is important.
He'll get you a basketful

of fried sparrow wings
with just enough crunch.
Don't be afraid

to eat the spicy, pickled
tongues; Saleem's mistress
ships them from Tripoli.

When the one-eyed beggar
visits your table for breadcrumbs,
give him the garlic-glazed liver.

He'll devour it;
you'll become sick
after the first bite. Wash you hands

before you swim;
the spices on your fingers
will attract the sharks.

FIRST VALENTINE (FOR AMARA ROSE)
ALYS MASEK

Conceived on Moelap, born on Majuro,
child of water, blue-green lagoon,
coral reefs and surreal colored fish.
You came to me across the International Date Line,
losing a day as you flew. I have a photo of you
the day you departed. You staring gravely
into the camera, eyes wide open,
your mother, only an arm clutching a manila envelope.

Your eyes are so dark they shadow blue;
your hair is black to my brown, thick,
and soft as the water from which you came.
"Amara" means "paradise" in Amharic,
though bitter were your beginnings.
Exhausted and jet-lagged you cried that first night,
until we curled up together on the big bed.
I changed and fed you and you brought me back
to that delirious baby world of walking and rocking,
watching the dawn unfold. Now, you hold out
your arms for mama, laugh at your sister as her blond
head bobs and weaves in a crazy bedtime dance.

How much will you keep of where you
began, that small island crowded with cinderblock
houses, the warm and sudden rain,
the words *yokwe, likatu, komol tata,*
the women with long dark hair, bright muumuus.
I wonder if the ocean will always
murmur in your ear, if any part of you still
stirs with the waves crashing against the reef.

HIGH TIDES
RHONA MCADAM

This time of year the tides are never higher:
eleven feet of water rise to the moon.
We rise and fall to some other power;
greedy for daylight, bodies wax and wane.

Eleven feet of water rise to the moon.
We wash ourselves in morning's river,
greedy for daylight. Bodies wax and wane.
We wonder what we've washed away forever.

We wash ourselves in morning's river,
swim free of our skin, we're buried at sea
and wonder what we've washed away forever.
Meet me a year from now: who will we be?

I've swum free of my skin; I'm buried at sea;
gone is the body you held with those hands.
Meet me a year from now: who will we be?
Measure your absence: make no demands.

Gone is the body you held with those hands.
I rise and fall to some other power,
measure your absence; make no demands.
This time of year the tides are never higher.

SIREN'S SONG (EXCERPT)
KATHLEEN McELLIGOTT

Reporter James Hudson

Ladies and gentlemen of Santa Fe, we're live this evening from the grand re-opening of a major art showcase under new ownership. Many more shows will start up in weeks to come, but this early opening of El Diablo Gallery— "The Devil,"—marks the start of the season. We have some "regulars" with us, Santa Fe artists like watercolorist Elaine McElroy, originally from Chicago; painters Ingrid Olson and Yvonne Rhodes; and a poet known simply as "Michael the Mountain Man," who's something of a local legend. He's known for his eye-catching outfits—from gold lamé evening wear to his Annie Oakley/Dale Evans-retro look—and his eye for the visual arts. He's a fixture at these openings, and if he's not in attendance, it's just not an event. Tonight he's wearing aubergine Spandex bike shorts and....

Elaine Mc Elroy

Michael's in his glory. He lives in a rickety shack in the foothills and looks more weathered every time I run into him. He's showing *a lot* of that skin tonight in purple-y black Spandex biker shorts, a Lycra jersey in chartreuse, and a Pepto-Bismol pink feather boa to top it off. Also his usual combat boots for protection from snakes and scorpions. Michael, you are a vision. You must be channeling Lance Armstrong tonight. Your abundant, curly chest hairs peek out from the partially unzipped Jersey City Bike-Psychos top.

I'm almost laughing out loud at Michael's latest reincarnation, but see a hand waving at me and it's Ingrid. Yvonne's with her, and when they come over, they're delighted to see my friend Christa, recognizing her from our hike up the Aspen Vista Trail. I introduce them to Trish as "Christa's partner—an artist in her own right," and they ooh and aah at her silver earrings, necklace and rings, which Christa proudly points out.

We're all talking about this lavishly catered event with flutes of champagne and hors d'oeuvres carried by handsome, uniformed waiters. Pitchers of garnet-colored sangria, white wines and sparkling water are on a side table. Salsa and blue corn chips, trays of raw veggies and dips, and colorful fruit platters surround the floral centerpiece accented with showy, bird-of-paradise flowers.

Heads turn as a young man in a tux calls for attention and the chatter subsides. "Welcome to El Diablo and its first show, kicking off the season. We're delighted this evening to exhibit some exciting regional paintings by previously undiscovered artists." Nobody's really listening, and people resume their conversations, though at half-volume. The guy finishes talking, and I hear murmurs of, "New owner... La Diva Martinez." The space suddenly quiets and the crowd parts like the Red Sea as a strikingly beautiful Latina in a form-fitting scarlet dress strides confidently down the center of the room. Her four-inch silver stilettos tat-tat-tat like a dangerous crack of lightening. To say she is breathtaking is an understatement; indeed, the breath of all the guests, men and women alike, is temporarily stilled.

A diva indeed! Ms. Martinez is none other than Mercedes, the notorious femme fatale who stole Christa's heart, lavished her with affection then tossed her to the curb when a new infatuation replaced her. I glance over to Christa who looks like she's been drained of all life-giving blood. Is Mercedes capable of that, too, I wonder?

Mercedes scans the crowd slowly. I have to admit, grudgingly, that she's even more beautiful than when I... when Christa and I first met her at my debut show in Chicago years ago. Tonight her dark hair is longer, hanging loosely over her smooth, mocha-colored shoulders and curling around her face with its to-die-for skin and high cheek bones. Was she always the enchanting temptress singing her siren's song?

Certainly, Christa saw it back then; all she could talk about was the electrifying Mercedes; how beautiful, accomplished and exciting— a flame of energy. For Mercedes it was just another conquest, her favorite kind since she was Christa's first woman lover. After less than a year it ended abruptly when Mercedes moved on to someone new.

Ironic, this unexpected reunion of the two former lovers—and in an art gallery—Mercedes' gallery. Not that Christa is an artist, she's a psychologist... it's Trish that creates beautiful jewelry. And speaking of Trish... she looks totally confused at Christa's stunned reaction to Mercedes, not to mention mine, since my mouth's probably hanging open. After all, Trish has never actually seen this dangerous and dangerously beautiful ex-lover—only heard about her from Christa.

Mercedes spots Christa among the guests and a flash of recognition registers as she immediately begins walking slowly, seductively, toward our little group. She's smiling and greeting other guests along the way, air-kissing both men and women. Who knows who's more taken by her celebrity—the men whose gazes inevitably drop to her voluptuous breasts threatening to spill over the deeply cut "V" of her neckline—or the women who seem dumbstruck either from jealousy or infatuation?

Christa Thompson

Oh my God, she's headed right towards me! I can't move, and she's suddenly here, larger than life, kissing both my cheeks and I'm in a spotlight, her spotlight. She takes a half-step back, assessing me at close range, and swoops down locking her lips on mine and pulling me toward her. The smell of her smoky perfume and the insistent pressure of her mouth send tidal waves throughout my body in places that have apparently been asleep—waves washing over me now like a tsunami. Damn you, Mercedes.

Trish Hoffman

Who is this woman sucking face with my partner? How dare she? How dare *they*…right in front of me…and everyone else who's gaping and aiming their cell phones, straining for a better shot. Is this a "show" at El Diablo? Performance art involving soul kissing? Did Christa and Elaine know about this? Every muscle in my body tenses for battle. I look to Elaine for support and she looks pale, almost shell-shocked. What the hell is going on? Christa pulls away from Spider Woman, takes a second to collect herself, and turns toward me, her face no longer chalky white, but flushed now, almost as red as Ms. Martinez' dress.

"Mercedes…Mercedes," she stammers, nervously clearing her throat, "this… is my partner, Trish." She stops, breathless. No wonder. "Trish is a silver artist and I'm wearing some pieces she's designed." She indicates the heavy silver necklace I made for her, marking our first anniversary.

I have no rational explanation for what happens next. Hurt and rage explode inside me and with a theatrical flourish I fling the glass of red wine I'm holding into Mercedes' face. She lurches backward instinctively as if to avoid the onslaught, but it's too late; the deep red liquid flows into her cleavage and drips down the front of her dress.

Elaine's mouth is open, but no words come out. Before anyone can react I grab her by the arm. "Come on," I say, "we are *so* out of here."

Christa Thompson

Appalled, I offer Mercedes the small cocktail napkin I'm holding while others gather around gawking, still aiming their cell phones at us, until her associate comes running with a roll of paper towels and a bottle of Evian.

"I've got to blot this with seltzer before it's ruined…it may be already." Mercedes seems calmer than I'd expect after having wine thrown in her face... by *my* partner. This type of thing has happened to her before, no doubt. I don't know whether to apologize for Trish or go after her, but she and Elaine are heading out the door. If I call to her, will she hear me?

"I'll need help getting the stain out... there's a bathroom in my office." Mercedes takes my arm and steers me toward the back of the gallery.

"Ms. Martinez, Ms. Martinez," the press calls after us. "A statement, please. Who was that woman who assaulted you? And who is this woman with you?"

A photographer with a press pass from *Santa Fe Spotlight*, an online newspaper, steps in front of us and snaps several pictures. Just what I *don't* need; photos of Mercedes and me splashed across the Internet—and in a newspaper, no less. In this tight knit-community it will likely go viral instantaneously—and what about my patients? My associates at work? I'm in way over my head. Way, way over—without a life jacket.

"Ms. Martinez, are you planning to press charges against your assailant?" He seems unduly gleeful, not to mention grateful; the "jealous girlfriend" angle is a much better story than the gallery opening.

Her Mona Lisa smile reveals nothing. "No comment." She steps in closer, taking me toward her private office.

—◇— —◇— —◇—

Mercedes locks the door behind us. Everything here is sleek and shiny; a glass top desk with chrome legs, oyster-colored carpet and a black leather sofa.

"Help me with my dress." She balances on one stiletto-clad foot, her hand on my shoulder for support, and pulls the damp dress off while pulling me down onto the sofa, laughing like we're a couple of kids and this is all a game. But it's no game.

She's wearing a red lace bra and matching thong that are quickly discarded onto the floor along with the dress. El Diablo, indeed. I don't even try to resist. Our bodies generate white hot energy and I dive into the overwhelming ocean of Mercedes. Everything is forgotten... Trish, the wine, Elaine, the crowd... everything.

—◇— —◇— —◇—

"Who are you calling—your little girlfriend? The one who doused me with my own wine in *my* gallery?" Her left eyebrow raises in question. "Needless to say *she's* permanently off my guest list." She scoops her bra and panties from the floor with her dagger-like nails, while I re-think calling Trish on my cell. No, maybe not. Best to speak with her in person. Besides, I'm still gasping, coming up for air.

"Stop it, Mercedes. She's my partner. We have a child together."

"Please—don't be getting all self-righteous with me. You didn't put up much of a fight; none at all, really. Tell me you were worried about her and your child while we were on the sofa." She opens the closet and selects a short black dress from several outfits conveniently hanging there. "Actually, your mousey friend did me quite a favor. I couldn't have asked for better PR if I'd planned it. Publicity like I'll be getting—like *we'll* be getting—costs thousands and it was dumped, literally, into my lap for free."

"I need to find her, make sure she and Deshy are alright."

"Go right ahead. I've got a gallery show to host." She rakes her nails through her lush hair then applies fresh lipstick, red, of course. Pausing with her hand on the doorknob, she looks directly at me, "You'll come back for more than just this quickie. Oh, and say hello to... Trina, is it? And tell her thanks. She's quite spirited. Is she that passionate in bed?"

Before I can say anything she's out the door, slamming it behind her. I'm astonished. Did this really happen... Mercedes and me making love in her office? Mercedes' ability to entice, tease and deliver seems even more powerful than before.

Now, though, guilt dampens the excitement of it all. And my heart—maybe I'm having a heart attack. An attack of heart is more like it.

Trish didn't wait around after the commotion—just took off and is probably packing to move in with Elaine, who's telling her what a skank I am; that she's better off without me, and Deshy, too, who deserves a better mom.

But when you stop and think about it, I was an innocent bystander. I didn't even know it was Mercedes' gallery until her grand entrance. She kissed *me*, and before I could explain or protest, Trish up and throws a glass of wine in Mercedes' face. That was the worst thing she could have done... that and walking out of the gallery. Doesn't she realize she played right into Mercedes' hands? Trish doesn't know her... how smart she is and what she's capable of. I'd say it's Mercedes-1, Trish-0, and I'm in negative numbers for sure.

Michael the Mountain Man

Everyone's staying, milling around, texting, which explains the newcomers streaming in, all to get a look at the re-emergence of Señora Mercedes, in something new and stunning, no doubt, as she comes out from her private lair with that blonde woman at her side. Both looking flushed with afterglow—ooh, la, la! That reporter's talking to people, taking more pictures and video, and the crowd is taking pictures of him taking pictures. With this bunch growing larger by the minute, the food won't last for long. Anyone not here is either sick or dead. At last! The reporter's done with those two who were talking with the blonde just before Mercedes made her grand entrance. I wonder... did they know about this lover's triangle? Oh, good; I'm the next to be interviewed for *my* take on the action, and I can honestly say, "I remember when" at the show a couple of years ago right here at this gallery when Porter, that cheap bitch, had it. I must say the food has vastly improved. Anyway, that Elaine person had a show of her paintings, one a gorgeous nude of a young man I still dream about, and mostly of the blonde and the little brunette. I'm guessing this Mercedes woman has a lot of history with those two. How best to say all this to Mr. Cute Reporter?

"Well, I can certainly say things have changed here along with the ownership, Mr. Hudson. You're with the *Santa Fe Spotlight*?" I fling my feather boa over my shoulder for emphasis, hoping he'll take my picture and headline it *Fashionista Speaks on Lovers' Spat at Gallery Opening*.

Christa Thompson

There's got to be a back door to this place. I'm certainly not walking out through that crowd with this disheveled look that screams, *SEX!* Folks will no doubt be thinking, *There she goes, Mercedes' latest conquest.* Now I understand the self-loathing some of my patients feel. I have to talk to Trish, make her understand it wasn't my fault. Once Mercedes spotted me in the crowd I was a goner. She locked onto me like a laser beam. If only Trish had stayed after the wine incident... defended me, fought for me. I didn't betray her... until she left my side.

There *is* a back exit, down a short hallway from Mercedes' office. A few more steps and I'm out of here without any further publicity, thank God. My colleagues at Mosaic Mental Health are not going to like this.

Just as I step out of the door short bursts of light bombard me, and I stumble over my own feet—damn these strappy sandals—almost toppling over. Oh my God, I'm standing under the back-door light, and someone's taking pictures, again. I'm in a fishbowl, drowning, going down for the third time!

A House Like None Other
Laurel Means

FOR SALE. BY OWNER. The hand-lettered sign made me swerve off Highway 51, braking just short of a ditch. Of all houses, out of the total number of houses in this small river town in the middle of Midwest prairies, the most unlikely. The most unusual. The most talked about. A *palace* of a house I'd known as a child and longed for. Dreamed about in the confused dreams during my childhood summers in that town – Nana's canning endless jars of green beans in Mason jars, a dog named Topsy, Pushkin the cat. The family sitting packed into the dark cool of the fruit cellar on a hot day. Waking up to doves mourning across the fields at morning's beginning. The cemetery's tall, whispering cedars, telling the secrets of grandparents, great aunts and uncles, long since covered only with memories.

That house at the end of our road. A house like none other, stately standing, aloof, inaccessible. Red brick, white gingerbread eaves, heavy green shutters, white-pillared porch. Its dimensions, fabric, architecture—ordinary Victorian. Not ordinary, however, was its square, glass tower. One would expect a widow's walk along the Atlantic coast. Why in Sangemon, with only a sluggish river down at the bottom of the hill?

I'd been looking for a house in some quiet town within commuting distance of the city. I'd had enough of stifling office cubicles, frustrating rush-hour traffic, noisy neighbors long into the night. In an agreement with my supervisor, I could set up a home office somewhere and come in only once a week. And so began the search.

That house up at the top of the hill in Sangemon. Bigger than I needed? Pricey? Something compelled me that afternoon to restart my Honda's motor and begin the climb up that main road to the top of the hill. Passing Nana's old house, I quickly turned my head away. The summer kitchen bulldozed over, only a mound where the fruit cellar had been. Shutters long since sold. A mobile home dominating the garden. A shattering of memories bringing only pain.

I tried to focus on that house at the end of the road. I allowed its weed-choked gravel driveway to beckon. I allowed the broken-down front porch steps to stop me, the overgrown cedar shrubs to entice me out of the car. I knew it was a whim. I was later to call it something else. Something like *coming home*.

A small portico jutted out from the front porch, its once white, wooden pillars streaked with cracks and peeling paint. A few floorboards were missing, weeds growing up through the gaps, an accumulation of dirt blown up against the door sill. Obviously useless to knock. The deadly quiet confirmed no one around. As I stepped back down off the porch, rationalizing this only as a whim, I smelled wood smoke. Thin, white wisps curled up from the chimney over the kitchen spur. Surely someone ... I knocked on the back door. After a long pause, it opened.

A gray-bearded man stood holding the door slightly ajar, said nothing until a dog inside started barking. "Quiet, Troy!" he shouted, then, "Well?"

"I've come about the house."

"What about it?"

"I might be interested in buying it."

"Buying it?"

"Yes–the sign said *For Sale by Owner*. Are you the owner?"

"What's that to you?"

Impossible man. "For sale or not? I'd like to have a look."

The door opened slightly more. "Might as well come in. Watch out for that dog, though. Don't like strangers."

The kitchen was a filthy shambles, cupboard doors hanging loose on hinges, counters littered with dirty dishes, muddy tracks crisscrossing broken linoleum, the pungent smell of something frying, a yellowish dog snarling. An old army cot in the corner suggested the man camped out in the kitchen.

The kitchen seemed a microcosm for the rest of the house–dirt, neglect, retrenchment, exclusion. The man led me through one empty room after another, grumbling as he opened an occasional shutter. Motes of dust floated in the few admitted sunbeams. An oppressive dampness, the pungent odors of age. Mingled scents of old leather, wood smoke from white-mantled fireplaces, spilling out their last ashes. There was no furniture except for a broken chair in one corner, an empty crate in another, a rusty bed spring leaning against the hall wall. Upstairs four large rooms opened out from a wide hallway, all silent, dark, except for one. That room had lost its inside shutters and late-afternoon sunlight reluctantly filled it. Dusty, empty, except for a large, old-fashioned rocking horse, its glassy eyes staring at me as if pleading for a small rider to ride off into a world filled with life. A reminder of my own lost childhood, Nana's house, down the road.

"Well, you've seen it," snapped the man. "Won't waste any more of your time." He headed down the stairway.

"Wait," I said. "Where do those small stairs go, end of the hall?"

"Them? Attic. Plain attic, like most old houses. Junk. Pigeon roost. Them stairs not safe."

"Can you get up to the glass tower through there?" That tower had held my imagination, even as a child. Strange, mysterious, odd.

He mumbled something, continued down the stairs. Nothing to do but follow him and try to get him to talk about selling. I knew I wanted that house. Perhaps it was the rocking horse. Fascination for the tower. The confusion of childhood dreams. Irrationality can seldom be explained.

Yet it was done. Mr. Pettigrew grudgingly agreed to my terms, although I sensed it was with a certain kind of relief. A month later I sat in the kitchen and looked around in frustration. The place still reeked of something frying–fish, maybe. Cupboard doors still hung from broken hinges. Linoleum still muddy, cracked, and broken. Most of my furniture was still in storage. I was camping out with a futon and two suitcases–not in the depressive kitchen, but in a corner of the dining room between the fireplace and elaborate, built-in buffet.

Where to begin to live? Truly and unequivocally live in that house? It seemed that everything needed restoration. I had a list of local handymen that seemed endless and expensive. It wasn't difficult—another irrationality—to long for the sanitized comfort of office cubicles, the confinement of an apartment, and, in the manifest silence of this vast house, the reassuring night-time sounds of other humans.

Admittedly, I was still enamored with the idea, a dream come true, despite the heaviness which seemed to hang fill each room like a physical presence. Even throwing open the shutters, one by one, letting light stream into patterns across the broad-beamed floor, failed to dispel it. The broken, derelict furniture symbolized broken lives, lives lost. The sense of loss often caught me feeling stiffled, oppressed, full of foreboding. Each time I went upstairs, the glassy eyes of the rocking horse looked more pleading than ever. Each time that narrow, broken stairway leading to the attic seemed more compelling. But the attic would have to wait, it wasn't essential. Sometimes, though, the feeling came that the stairway, the attic—and beyond, *were* essential.

"I imagine, ma'am, you'll want to start with this here kitchen," said the local man I'd finally hired. "Hub of the house, they always say."

"You're probably right, Seth. At least the previous owner lived in here. Like some more coffee?"

"No thanks, ma'am." He set down this mug. "Yup, a real recluse, you might say. Once offered to help him fix up a few things, but nothin' doin'."

"Lived here long?"

"Most his life, I guess. Parents 'fore him, goes way back."

"They couldn't have built the house."

"Nope, couple of families 'fore that. Came here from someplace out East." He pushed back his chair, picked up his wooden tool tote. "If you'll excuse me, miss, I'd best get busy. Start with them cupboard doors?"

Someplace East. The widow's walk on top of the house. Things were beginning to come together. Several days later I talked to Mary's son, proprietor of the general store down by the river. "What can you tell me about that house up there?" I asked.

"Hmm, not much, Joan," she replied, bagging the last of my few groceries. "Folks up there—not much to do with any of us. Ever. To tell you the truth, we never were eager for it. Always seemed to have bad luck; 'fraid it might rub off."

"What kind of bad luck?"

"Oh, things like babies dyin', accidents. Old Jim Pettigrew had a couple brothers. Last one killed, thrown off his paw's tractor while they were out plowin' one day. Prob'ly ten years old or so. Then after the old folks passed away, Jim stayed on. Tried to keep up with the farmin'—mostly corn. Soon couldn't manage. Just let that old house go to pot. Shame, really. Beautiful old house like that. Must be a curse or somethin' on it."

I couldn't help but smile on my way home. *A curse on that house.* The stuff of gothic novels, stereotyped mystery stories. Was I going to find a skeleton in the attic? Accidents—deaths—all happen. Surely only human instinct to connect, identify, find explanations.

Next day two men arrived for the roof. "Got to get that attic stairway repaired 'fore the men start up there," Seth had said. After several days of ripping and pounding, Webber called me up to inspect. It was the first time I'd been up those narrow stairs.

An attic like any other? How disappointing. A large, dusty space under steeply dropping rafters, old chairs, unidentified junk. "Come up to the tower, Miss, you'll see better," came Seth's voice. "Here, I'll give you a hand."

A ladder led up to the tower from the center of the attic, a trap door at the top. I needed his hand to manage the last two rungs and climb over the sill.

The view was breathtaking, the feeling of being so high, protected only by glass, frightening. I steadied myself by holding onto a projecting piece of corner molding. Something caught my eye–no, not just a piece of Victorian gingerbread molding. Something–a dolphin, upright on its tail, my hand on its fin. A dolphin in each corner.

Standing in that glass enclosure I could look all the way down Main Street, past the ruin of Nana's house, all the way to the river. Other directions revealed miles of fields of corn, alfalfa, pastures, clumps of cottonwood, patches of green prairie grass. The tower's glass door stood open, a strong wind blowing through.

"Looks fine," I shouted above the wind. For some reason I suddenly felt lightheaded, dizzy, unsure of my footing. Now the glass walls seemed not even to exist. I sensed I was floating in space. I reached out ... the dolphin stared at me, its gaping mouth laughing ...

"Wait," he called back. "Let me help you down. Don't want another accident."

"Another accident?" his arm steadied me until my foot touched the first stair. I waited as he shut the tower door, and we both continued downstairs.

"What accident?" I remembered Mary's comments in the general store.

"Guess you never heard that story, even though you grew up over in Mason City." He paused, laughed. "Don't know if it's true or not, you know how folks' imagination works. Might make you feel different 'bout this old house."

"I doubt it," I said, sounding more convinced than I actually was. "But I'm here to stay, my family, too, when and if I have one." I had to make those rooms come alive, fill them with sounds and sunlight, fill them with anything to bring them back.

"Good lookin' gal like you," he said with a grin. "Won't be long. Well, anyways, 'bout that accident. Happened long, long time ago, hundred years or so. Must've been three, maybe four years after this house was built. Those Pettigrews came from somewhere out East. Place on the coast, fishing fleet. One day Captain Pettigrew, he never came back. Lost in a storm. Left his widow, two or three sons. Then another winter, another storm, another ship lost, another son. This time the eldest son, believe Peter was his name, decided no more of the sea. So's he bought some prairie land–far away from the sea. Probably several hundred acres, back in those days a good part of Sangemon. Only it wasn't all settled yet, see."

"Was he the one who built this house, then? Peter Pettigrew?"

"The one. Well, he had his widowed mother, his widowed sister Abigail, maybe another brother–not sure."

"The accident?"

"That's the strange thing. Nobody ever sure whether an accident or not. What people say, was this. Pettigrew's sister, Abigail, never got over her grief. You see, when he built this house, he had it built just like the one they had back East. His sister'd go up to that tower, just like the women-folk used to do back there, watching the sea for the first sign of their menfolk. She'd spend most of her time up there, toward the end refuse to come down to eat. Slept up there sometimes. People said she'd be shouting something, crying."

"Shouting? Like what?"

"Dunno, but they sure thought she'd gone crazy with grief. Nobody seemed to be able to do anything. Just as well. Nature took care of itself."

"Nature? Meaning what?"

"Well, the feeling was she got so crazy she didn't know what she was doing. She just crashed through the glass and slid down off the roof. Broke her neck, story goes." He drained his mug of coffee, pushed back the chair. "Must be leavin' and get home to finish a few chores 'fore dark. Be back tomorrow, start on the barn roof. Got plans for that barn? Could rent it out as storage space, I guess."

After Seth left, I found it hard to concentrate on plans for the next project, the roofless barn. It was because of Abigail. What was the state of her mind before she crashed through the glass? How could we ever know? An imaginative urge engrosses any story. And my mind, in that engrossment, was up in the look-out tower with Abigail.

Yes, I—Abigail—was there, looking out over the rippling green of prairie grasses, the billowing green waves of the sea, waiting, waiting. Feeling the salty sea wind on my face, rustling my dress, driving the sail coming toward me, coming home. I could wait no longer. I gathered my full skirts around me. I could see only the sea, his ship. I plunged into the waves of that green grass sea to meet him. We would come home together.

I, SALMON

KARLA LINN MERRIFIELD

Thirsting to arrive at my source,
I find first fast cascades, white boils,
then slow, silent meanderings.
I fin from boisterous canyon river
to broad meadow slough stillness
in an imperceptible current.
I lunge upstream many mountain miles,
remembering the nacreous egg
from which I came, & I spawn
a million red pearls in a rush of water.
The cells swell in answer & take
from me my body of life.

ON SEAGULLS
LYLANNE MUSSELMAN

I have to live near seagulls.
I don't know why—being born
and bred in land-locked Central Indiana,
but my favorite vacations, and
now where I live near Lake Erie—
gulls rule. They make me happy.
Some people despise these gulls
as dirty, pesky scavengers—
rats with wings. I see them
as freedom, laughter,
warm memories, the promise
of sunny days. These majestic birds
with angel wings in flight, their
constant caws and squeals are a delight
when I see them swooping low
over Toledo - in Metroparks, over city streets,
floating on the Maumee River,
gathered in massive congregations
on the beach before flying away—
flashing the public
their energetic sermons.

Taking Out the Dock

R.J. Nelson

Long after the neighbors' piers are pulled,
mine still serves for walks over water,
temporary bridge to freshwater dreams.
I put off takeout until flurries fall
and broom fog sweeps the lake clean,
until the last boats leaving for winter berths
blow down the lake like heat guns,
peeling back the surface
for a new coat of ice.

Then I wade out to the deep end
and brace against those foaming wakes
that curl and slap chest high,
sloshing over the best of boots.
I raise my arms and shout, "Slow down,"
but in lake fog what's the use?
I have to hurry and time my chore—
to lift before the next boat roar,
another length of dock to shore.

106

ROMEO CORPEN

VON PITTMAN

Almost two dozen officers and enlisted men stood on the hangar deck at the open, fifty-foot door of Elevator 1, watching three dolphins leap and dive precisely halfway between the old Midway-class aircraft carrier *USS Coral Sea* (CVA-43), and the even older fleet oiler *USS Passumpsic* (AO-107), off to starboard. The Elevator 1 door provided a safe place to stand and get a good view of the dolphins. The sailors on the bridges and in the engine rooms of the two ships worked with intense concentration and quick reflexes to set, then maintain, the ordered constant speed and direction, a synchronous course called the *Romeo Corpen*. It was an unusually pleasant, breezy November Saturday morning on Yankee Station, the carrier staging area in the Tonkin Gulf, at 17 degrees 30 minutes north, 108 degrees 30 minutes east. The course was 195 degrees, the speed precisely 14 knots. The Officers of the Deck of the two ships had to maintain an exact spacing of 180 feet in order to keep the proper tension on the latticework of lines, spanwires, and hoses linking their vessels.

Underway replenishment operations—UNREPS—require skilled seamanship and intense concentration. This is especially true when a carrier takes on fuel, ordnance, and supplies. The carrier's size and massive flight deck overhang make close-order maneuvering difficult. Because of their size and shape, carriers are slow to respond to—or "answer"—orders to change course and speed. Coming alongside an oiler, receiving the lines and hoses, then maintaining constant course, speed, and spacing demands as much concentration and skill as are expended during flight operations. Perhaps UNREPS demand even greater skill. Collisions between two ships are unlikely during flight ops. When refueling, they are a constant threat.

The dolphins appeared unconcerned with the rigors of course and speed. They maintained a perfect fourteen knots, swimming in a straight line, ninety feet from each ship. Their navigation seemed effortless, maybe even mocking. To humans, dolphins always appear to be smiling. They don't smile, of course. But that day they induced smiles from many of the men standing at Elevator 1 and from those manning the fueling stations.

During Tonkin Gulf UNREPS, two officers and about six or seven enlisted men stood on each fueling platform, spaces of roughly 10 x 15 feet under the flight deck overhang, and crowded with receiving pipes, winches, hoses, and block and tackle.

A junior officer—an Ensign or Lieutenant Junior Grade (LTJG)—from the Engineering Department and two enlisted Boilermen were there to see to the receiving of fuels. The Coral Sea required massive amounts of NSFO (Navy Special Fuel Oil) to run its antiquated, World War II, 600-pound steam propulsion system, while its airplanes ran on kerosene-based JP-5 (Jet Propulsion-5). The Deck Department assigned an Ensign or LTJG as "Safety Officer" on each platform. He and four enlisted men from the Deck Division attended to the winches, tensioners, and rigging.

The key man on the platform, however, was usually a second- or third-class Bosun's Mate, also from the Deck Department. He was the "rig captain," responsible for keeping the proper tension on the wires and lines supporting and controlling the fueling hoses.

The "rig captain" wore a yellow hardhat. The Safety Officer's was white with a green cross, and the winch operator's was brown. Engineers wore gray hardhats. All wore bright orange life preservers. The dolphins required no safety equipment.

Enlisted men did all the work on the fueling platform. The two junior officers mainly tried to stay out of their way. Their job was to stand there for four or five hours with no trips to the head and no smoke breaks. They would come into play only if something went seriously wrong. One of the Navy's oldest clichés is, "Somebody's got to hang." If a man fell overboard or a coupling gave way and thousands of gallons of NSFO were spilled, someone with a little rank had to be deemed responsible. He, or they, would face a court of inquiry, and perhaps a court-martial.

The two officers stood toward the back of the platform (against the ship's hull) and tried to remember to flex their knees frequently. They did their best not to think about it as their nicotine fits grew in intensity. But even for them, this UNREP was better than usual. They, too, could see the three dolphins.

Unlike the sailors on the fueling platforms, the men looking out from Elevator 1 did not need to be there. Some should have been at work; others could have been in their racks, resting up for their next watch on the bridge, in an engine room, in the galley, or in dozens of other work spaces. But they stood there, watching. A couple brought out Super-Eight movie cameras. Several ran for the expensive Japanese single-lens-reflex cameras that most Seventh Fleet sailors seemed to believe they were required to bring home. They shot whole rolls of KODACHROME slide film, trying over and over to catch the dolphins at the tops of their leaps.

Many "short-timers"—both enlisted men and officers—had not only become jaded about the Vietnam War and the Navy, but prided themselves in having done so. But for a few hours, in the shallowest corner of the South China Sea, they couldn't feel jaded. The dolphins' beauty and elegance overcame the sailors' affected indifference.

The dolphins didn't seem to tire. Well into their second hour of synchronized swimming with two U.S. Navy ships, they continued to leap, sometimes one after the other, sometimes simultaneously. "How do they *do* that," the sailors occasionally asked each other. Frequently, men simply said in awed, subdued voices, "Fucking beautiful."

While the *Romeo Corpen* held, nothing broke the mood. The ship-bound mammals respected and admired the unfettered mammals in the water. Sailors had once considered the company of dolphins good luck. But by 1969, superstition was no longer what it had been, at least in the Western Pacific. Now the dolphins were an elegant and entertaining—but transient—diversion from the normal mix of boredom and nervous tension endemic on combatant ships. Even the junior officers on the fueling platforms had forgotten the remote possibility of courts-martial.

At the end of Yankee Station UNREPS, the captains of the ships frequently agreed to conduct emergency breakaway drills. Ships linked together by numerous lines and hoses, locked into a *Romeo Corpen*, would be sitting ducks for enemy ships and airplanes. Therefore, the Navy has always considered it critical that crews be trained to rapidly break all connections. Emergency breakaway drills do not allow the omission of any of the usual steps in securing supply operations; crews are expected to perform all prescribed steps, but more quickly. Either way, however, it is not a fast process. To speed it up significantly would almost certainly result in fatal accidents. In the Tonkin Gulf, emergency breakaway drills always reminded the crews that they should be grateful the North Vietnamese had neither submarines nor an air force. The drills had been useful in World War II. On Yankee Station in the 1960s, they were irrelevant.

The captains of the *Coral Sea* and the *Passumpsic* used the telephone line that is always passed over during UNREPS to set a precise time to commence their emergency breakaway drill. But the dolphins unilaterally broke off the *Romeo Corpen* two minutes before the call for the drill sounded from the 1-MC loudspeaker systems of both ships. The watchers at Elevator 1 drifted away. The platform crews secured their operations quickly and carefully.

Within ten minutes after securing from the emergency breakaway drill, the *Passumpsic* had set a course for Subic Bay, Philippines, to take on another load of NSFO and JP-5. It would return to Yankee Station in three days. The *Coral Sea*'s crew prepared for air ops; the first launches would commence in two hours. Where the dolphins were, nobody knew. Breaking off the *Romeo Corpen* had been easy for them. The sailors liked to think the dolphins were still smiling. But they knew better.

Tangling with Spruce
Susan Pope

I've followed Jim, the man I plan to marry, to this river. I trust him. He's a field biologist with plenty of raft and wilderness experience. I'm a single mother who's never paddled a raft. He has arranged the whole trip.

A float plane drops four of us off at Judd Lake, the headwaters of the Talachulitna River in Southcentral Alaska. We will take out in six days, just below the rapids. For ten years Skip, Jim's college buddy, has been lusting after the Tal, a world-famous fly-fishing destination. Louise, his long-time partner, joins us.

In Skip's fishing magazines, the Tal runs clear, cold, and fast. But now, in early June after a late spring, we discover a meaner, dirtier version of the Tal. Trees yanked from banks at break-up. Mangled limbs, broken logs, chunks of earth and roots all swirl in the chocolate water.

I scrape my thumb knuckle—again—against the side of the raft. The cold freezes the pain for a few seconds before the burn starts. The knot above my right shoulder blade throbs and my biceps have turned to jelly.

I'm in the bow straddling the wet rubber tube in my hip waders that are cinched to my belt, one foot pleasantly cool in the icy brown water, the other cramped and sweaty jammed into the toe hole at the bottom of the raft. Butt cheeks wrap tightly around the slowly deflating rubber pontoon. Jim is not the expert I thought he was. We are not a paddling team. We careen against snags and boulders, twist around, head down-river backwards.

"Paddle deeper," he says. "Quit splashing water on me."

I try but can't seem to find the rhythm. It doesn't help that our raft grows more flaccid as the day wears on. At Judd Lake we inflated each raft with the foot pump the flight service provided. Huff. Huff. Huff. Then, a slow steady *hiss* escaped from our boat. We splashed lake water on the rubber in search of leaking air. An old patch on the outer pontoon gurgled. We pulled out the patch kit. Empty. No glue, no patches, nothing but a bag of cellophane and empty tubes left by the last people to rent this raft.

I blame him. He didn't check the raft, the company, the gear. He should know how to steer this sagging rubber duck. I blame myself for once again trusting a man more than I trust myself, for believing that if he says he knows something, he does. Maybe he's not who I thought he was. Maybe I shouldn't expect a man to take care of me. Maybe I should learn to take care of myself.

On Day Two the river requires more precision than we can muster. Skip and Louise soar ahead with their robust raft and years of experience. Finally, we conquer a sharp dog-leg in the river, and I think we're catching on. But, dead ahead, a massive spruce spans the river, funneling the flow to a narrow channel on the opposite side.

"Back paddle," Jim screams. "Hard! Goddamit."

The sluggish raft drifts on, gliding with the river's inevitable flow.

"Paddle! Hard! Hard! Goddamn it! Paddle!"

Pull. Pull. Pull. My bony arms cannot withstand the churning current. It sucks us toward the spruce like water down a flushing toilet, until we are caught. The raft begins to buckle as the river surges beneath the tree.

"Jump!" Jim yells.

"What?" I scream above the roar.

"Get the hell out!"

He's crazy. We're in a hole. It's deep. Five minutes is all you have in water this cold. But something about his voice makes me obey him.

I slip over the edge and slide into the frigid water. It floods my nose, scrapes my scalp like a blade, and stuns my heart, ceasing all movement in my limbs, whirling me like a chunk of driftwood. Then my cheap yellow life jacket takes over and pops my head above the surface. But my water-filled hip waders hold me suspended in the river.

This is not how I'm going to die.

A fat root just below the surface protrudes from the undercut bank. I kick my leaden legs and grab for the slippery piece of wood. I catch it. My spindly arms grow fierce and powerful. Hand-over-hand, inch-by-inch, I drag my body up the base of the tree until I can heave one knee up onto the bank, then the other. I crawl to a mat of spongy moss and slowly rise to my feet. Unsnapping and peeling down my boots, a gush of water washes out and puddles at my feet.

"Where are you?" Jim yells from below me.

"Over here."

I lean out over the bank, one hand clamped to a willow, thinking he is caught in the water. But no, he stands mid-river on the trunk of the downed tree.

"The raft is gone," he yells. "You have to walk the tree across the river."

"What?" My brain is still underwater.

"The raft's pinned under the tree. You have to get to the other side of the river with Skip and Louise."

Hypothermic shivers take over. I stumble toward his voice and peer into the river at the same log that claimed the raft a lifetime ago. I must grab hold of a limb, pull myself onto the spruce trunk, and step around the protruding spikes to reach the other side. My legs are not capable of this feat.

A great thrashing and crackling occurs below me. In a flash of blue and yellow, Jim crashes from the river through the willows and grabs my hand.

"I thought you went under with the raft," he says. "I didn't know where you were."

His eyes are wide. He pulls my soaking body to his chest. The buckles on our life jackets click and scrape.

"Come on. We've got to find our gear."

He grips my elbow and leads me to the bank. Together we climb into the broken spruce and thread our way across the river, leaping the few feet from the crown of the tree to the opposite bank.

On shore, Louise builds a teepee of twigs, grass, and driftwood, and nurtures a tiny flame. She lays dry pants and shirt on a rock as the fire takes off.

"Strip." She says. "You've got to warm up."

Calm, sensible, grounded Louise. I sit on a rock, wriggle out of my boots, shamelessly peel off my clothes, and climb into the dry warmth of her pants and sweatshirt. I rub my hands together over the fire and begin to thaw. As the blood returns to my brain and extremities, our predicament sinks in. One raft, four people, half the gear, half the food, four more days until our pick-up downstream from the rapids. As far as we know, there's no one else on the river.

Jim and Skip spend hours standing crotch-deep in the river at the toe of a gravel bar retrieving gear flung free from the raft. Sleeping bags, pads, day packs, tent, intact, but wet in their river bags. Finally, the power of the current flushes the raft from beneath the tree. The men haul it to our makeshift camp and we unpack the food still lashed to the boat in a waterproof bin. We inventory our gear: cookies and crackers turned to mush. Freeze-dried packets intact. Jim's camera destroyed (a pin-prick hole in the case that held it). Lost: one case of beer and our only pump.

Over a pot of macaroni and cheese and fried soggy fig bars we replay the scenes from the day over and over, blaming the flight service for the bum raft, and ourselves for believing they checked it. Jim and I accept equal blame for inept paddling. As the fire dies our options dwindle to two: stay put and hope that someone comes along with a patch kit and pump, or continue down river in the morning with hopes of finding help. We decide to keep moving.

In our tent, Jim and I kick off our shoes and slide fully clothed into clammy sleeping bags. Midnight sun filters through the blue walls of the tent, now nearly dry, casting our skin in a pale somber wash. We draw the nylon bags to our chins.

"I thought you were gone," he says.

"You told me to jump in the river."

"The raft was buckling."

"You saved my life." Amazed at my body's power to survive, I think, *I saved myself.*

"What will we do without a pump?" Jim wonders.

"Fuck the river. I want to go home."

"We could have died," he says.

"Yeah."

He reaches over, unzips my sleeping bag and pulls my sweatshirt over my head. We take off our clothes and hold each other skin to skin, not with passion, but as two survivors seeking comfort from each other.

"I should have checked the raft myself before we left," he says for maybe the tenth time.

I shouldn't trust you completely, I think, but I don't say it. I can't afford to take these chances, to leave my daughter to be raised by her father. Trust should be given sparingly, sifted carefully through your own good sense and reasoning, not dumped wholesale onto someone else.

"The raft won't have enough air to make it through the rapids," he whispers.

"There have to be other people on the river. We'll find them."

Outside, the river rushes on, jostling rocks like some invisible giant playing in the shallows. Exhausted, we fall asleep, two warm bodies crammed into one damp sleeping bag, our futures already spreading and tangling together like the roots of an old spruce.

FRIED WATER
LYNN VEACH SADLER

Tankers, three-four million gallons
of crude oil per . . . .
Dozens of . . . .
Flaming crude . . . .
Smoldering wrecks . . . .
Burning bodies . . . .
The smell—*stench* . . . .
Fried *sealife*—fried *life* . . . .
Infernos . . . .
Oil-soaked beaches . . . .
Purpled globs that won't bear thinking. . . .

Six-months' assault
before Admiral Doenitz
called a halt,
ordered his six remaining
prowling submarines—U-boats—
away from the Atlantic Coast's Outer Banks
to other Hunting Grounds.
The sea-air defense had become too great.

And besides, all the water,
all that went with the water,
was fried.
Fried water.

DEBAUCHERY

PAUL SALUK

Our beaches smell like car engines. The waters
shiver. An assault of non-stop

insults crack the ocean floor and release
the crude that lies beneath.

Lakes slimed with a rainbow sheen of oil
deceive the death below.

Inland, used beer cans, condoms, and lunch bags disrespect
the springs I enjoyed since
before I was old.

For now   I turn inward.
Scent saturates my nostrils like nectar
soaks the hummingbird's beak.

HIGH BANK CANTO IV (2107)
GEORGE SAMERJAN

Mild ocean swells rocking us like the arms of a loving mother,
rumbling engine below us singing a deep-throated lullaby,
and we coursing a gently swaying course across the sea,
a dark object,
still touched with the night's cover and not yet revealed by dawn slipped
in a half-glimpsed arc beneath the waves,
mirage perhaps,
trick of the sea or something to come,
portent, messenger, or spirit,
and perhaps no difference among the three,
the first neared us,
then a pair,
then dozens, hundreds
of sleek, dark porpoises surrounded the *Booby Hatch*,
beneath the bow,
off the stern,
sliding down the keel,
they danced and skipped through sea and sky,
slipping silently beneath the froth-splattered waves only to surface,
for hours they stayed the course,
an abundance of moving, graceful life around us,
one after another these curious beings closed on us,
sometimes gazing or winking before disappearing beneath the sea,
allowing us to be with them.

Crossing the North Sea
Nancy Scott

I've forgotten the name for that kind
of storm, but it hardly matters.
I think of it as God having had
a really bad temper tantrum.

Our little ferry boat was cursed.
A test of its faith? Or payback
for some grievance God thought up
to harass seafaring vessels.

What had those poor horses done
to deserve such a fate?

Contentedly tethered in the hold until the sea
rose up, thirteen purebred
Arabians, pride of a Saudi prince,
broke loose.

Past midnight, it wasn't a dream
as I lurched along corridors, desperate
for crackers stashed in my car below
to blunt the relentless nausea.

That's when I saw the gaping wound aft,
heard the crew yelling, some wielding
grappling hooks, some clinging
to the rail peering down, impotent
as the last horse disappeared.

THREE WORLDS
(AFTER M.C. ESCHER)
DON SEGAL

Swallows skim the pond
Dip and dive
For insects in soft rain.

Ever was there a fish
That snapped at the surface
But grabbed feathers for a meal?

And the swallow,
Pulled below for a minute,
How strange.

Could I reach out to you
And pull in a kernel
Of what flows between us?

I would cradle it for a while,
Then let it float back,
How strange.

120

WATER WASHES AWAY ALL SINS
GRAZINA SMITH

Squinting, I shake my head as I lie immobile on the same bed my mother died in and watch the sun's rays flash through the apple blossom branches, slowly drifting across the whitewashed bedroom wall. I woke this morning and couldn't move, helpless, my limbs useless, but my mind sharp as ever. Memories of my life float before me as clearly as the sunlight on the wall. A smell of sage wafts through the window and its spiciness brings back recollections of that night. It was hot then, too, and the air was pungent with sage. I had been sitting up in bed for hours, sweaty and tense, and the headboard dowels had worn red furrows in my back. I could hear my mother Emma's labored breathing; it told me she was awake, too. Her voice had become only a whisper and I had moved into her bed to hear her if she needed me at night. We both knew she was dying. Each morning, when I opened my eyes, I held my breath frightened that the room would be still, that I would no longer hear her ragged struggle.

I always believed Emma and I were close, and can remember our many winter evenings together when we read the weekly paper from cover to cover more than once. The mailman came out to the ranch on horseback twice a month to deliver our mail but, when the heavy snows fell, his trips stopped until spring. We stacked each weekly newspaper on a kitchen chair and tried to solve the crossword puzzles during the long winter months. We were never clever enough to do it. The words we chose seldom fit the spaces and our erasures finally tore holes in the page. We'd check the answers in the following week's edition and they made sense but the new puzzle again proved impossible. As a child, I once got a 500-piece jigsaw puzzle from Emma for Christmas. For days, I tried to copy the drawing on the box but all I could finish was the frame and then only because the flat side of each piece gave me a clue to its position. I asked Emma for help but she was no better. We sorted and handled those pieces until our sweaty hands had misshapen the edges. They were like Indian drawings on the canyon walls. We couldn't make sense of them because we didn't have the key.

I guess this shows that neither one of us was very cunning, so it seems strange that we so easily got away with murder. It must be because women are considered incapable of brutal crimes, as if those crimes are against our nature. When we kill, we're expected to use poison or maybe a gun. I cut Sam's throat as he lay in bed in a drunken stupor. I had butchered enough hogs so I knew what to expect.

Once the plan to kill Sam formed in my mind, I knew I would carry it out. On that hot night, I went to his bedroom naked, leaving my nightgown outside the door. Sheriff Bradley would look for blood stains on clothes or maybe check to see if they were wet from recent washing. I only had one nightgown and a few dresses for him to inspect. Sam's blood spurted and covered both the wall and me, but he never woke and I don't think he suffered. It was an unexpected kindness I gave him in death. Afterward, I washed the knife and myself in Beaver Creek, then wrapped the knife in newspaper and buried it in the hog pen. A good knife was hard to come by in those days. I slept soundly until dawn.

My only mistake, if you can call it that, turned out to be the ornate pewter button with a star-burst design that I pressed into Sam's hand as he lay dying. Since my husband whored all over the county, I didn't think the sheriff would find its owner. I wanted to throw suspicion on an outsider, someone passing the ranch. Earlier in the week, I'd found the button glinting in the straw on the floor of the wagon and kept it because I had so few pretty things. It helped save me and condemned another.

Sam always went into town to buy supplies and I would unload the wagon when he returned. I could heft fifty-pound bags of feed or flour as easily as most women lifted a baby. Very few things made me uneasy but I never liked going into town and never understood the rules there. It seemed to me that people used civility and manners to entice bits of private pain from me for their own gossip and amusement. I was glad to have Sam run the errands.

The morning after Sam died I went into town to get Sheriff Bradley. We lived almost ten miles away on Beaver Creek right along the bend where it splits from the Green River. My mother's family homesteaded this valley and she was born in this house and lived here all her life as I hoped to do. I never knew my father. Neither Emma nor I made good choices in men. Emma married a drifter and he was gone before I was born. She told me very little about him.

When I was young, I did some foolish things myself and my marriage to Sam was one of them. Sam was a drinker and a brawler with a mouth full of sweet stories that made his life seem exciting. After a few months of marriage, I knew I'd made a mistake and returned home. Sam followed me. He immediately saw the advantage of a ranch near the bend of a great river, a place he hoped to one day call his own, and even my sharp tongue could not chase him away. Sam was like a tick, burrowing and sucking my strength. Sometimes I feared only my shell would remain when he finished. Of course, I didn't kill him because he was slowly draining my life. The very rhythm of that act leads to fatigue, not hatred or anger.

It started when, for almost a week, Sam came home sweaty and dirty. I was surprised because he never did hard labor around the ranch. I finally had to ask where he'd been, what he was doing. "I've dammed Beaver Creek and flooded the south pasture," he said. "Why ever did you do that?" I asked him. The reason for his actions, his callousness, stunned me. Sam knew Emma was dying and he planned to sell the ranch after she passed away. The dam would demonstrate the value of our land. Beaver Creek flowed through our holdings before it watered the ranches downstream. Sam wanted eager buyers. With the dam, drought threatened our neighbors and they came harassing me and pleading with Emma. What could she do on her death bed? "Give me some peace and rein in that man." She croaked. "Are you gonna let him destroy everything we've worked for?" She prodded me every time I entered her room.

Emma knew my greatest joy is this ranch. Often, I ride up the bluffs to look down on the valley. Even now, in bed, I can see it in my mind's eye. The creek meanders like a green ribbon dropped by a careless girl. From the heights, the green strand of cottonwoods is thin until the eye rests on the ranch. There the color expands to a fertile crescent produced by the labor and sweat of three generations. My mother planted an apple tree outside our front door and I grew up with it. From a distance, it marks the house; its branches reflect the seasons. Springtime blossoms are a pale mist against the cabin. Summer sees it blend with its lush surroundings and, in early fall, apples are bright red flecks spattered on a canvas of leaves. I used to like it best in winter. After I'd checked the v-slot canyon where we confined our cattle, I'd ride slowly back and see the tree's bare branches against the glimmers of light from the windows. That was my welcome home to Emma and supper. At night, the wind tapped the branches against the cabin, rapping like the skeletal knuckles of ancestral ghosts.

Sam knew how much I love this land. He knew I would die if I had to leave it, but he only cared about the money the ranch would bring. I could think of only one solution and Emma's goading encouraged me. Today, women probably can't understand my desperation. They would get a lawyer, get a divorce or have Emma make a will. It's hard to remember those helpless times and impossible to understand hopelessness until you've lived it. Sam could sign my name to any paper and no one would question it or listen to my stammered protests. There would be plenty of men—lawyers, even judges—eager to get our land and, thereby, side with him. I raged to Emma that our lives meant so little until my rage turned against the cause of my pain with a force I was surprised to find within me.

That afternoon, when I returned with the sheriff, the very violence of the crime made him suspect an outsider. Also, my mother swore that I had not left her side all night. Sheriff Bradley knew Emma all his life. She was an honest woman. He told us Sam had a fight during his last trip to town. Matt Hobson attacked him over the creek dam. Of course, it was Matt's button that landed on our wagon among the bags of feed.

As I lie helpless here this morning, the sun dips further down my wall and I can hear the chickens squawking in their pen. They're enclosed to keep them safe from coyotes and I can't feed them today. My visitors are few and it will be a while before they're fed again. They'll start to peck each other and turn against the weakest member. That's what happened to Matt Hobson.

Matt was the spoiled son of a rich man and he was always causing trouble in town. There were so many stories about his short temper that people looked at Matt and believed he could kill a man, especially over water. The minister preaches that water washes away our sins but we know, in a parched land, water causes more sins than it washes away. Matt argued and protested, but he was as effective as a rabbit in the clutches of a hawk. His father swore he was home, but people told each other that Old Man Hobson had protected his son once too often. Matt Hobson went to prison for the murder. Years later, he came back to visit me. I don't know if he came to proclaim his innocence or if he suspected me of the crime and hoped for a confession. We sat on my front porch, our long uncomfortable silence broken by comments on the weather and the price of feed, until he finally sighed, stood up and left. I heard he settled in Kansas City, a broken man, but I never felt deep regret about my choices. I accepted the cards fate dealt me, made the best of them and played the hand to my advantage. The pewter button led to a suspect but, in the end, the killing also caused a second confession. My one strong regret is that I heard that confession.

I was overwhelmed when Emma lied to Sheriff Bradley and told him I spent all night with her. I thought her death-bed voice carried the weight of love, that she understood me well and knew my jagged edges could only fit in this place. Later, when I clumsily tried to thank her, I learned our bond was more primitive than love. She whispered that she knew how things like that can happen, that my father lay under the roots of the apple tree. I was shocked into silence and she died that day before I could recover and ask her more. For a lifetime, unanswered questions crowded my mind. I could never bring myself to cut the tree and, through the years, each fall the apples rotted around the cabin. I wouldn't even feed them to the pigs.

As I lie here now the room is filled with the orange glow of sunset and the air begins to reek with the ghostly smells of spoiled cider and my compromised dreams.

Always, Always the Water Rushes On—
Julie Stuckey

a powerful plash and roar down mountainside
in a cold churning past rock and tree,
foaming, swirling, eddying, joining, tumbling,
an onrush following no path other than
now — pouring itself again and again.

Like mountain shamans using ancient woodblocks
to imprint prayers onto water, my thoughts
join this river, these stones, this earth;
become spill over boulders, reflected light of day,
onrush of spirit, breath, moment — death a mere
disappearance,   ripples in the flow.

FROST MOON

INGRID SWANBERG

if you look
straight across the lake
where the glittering water below the sun
meets the line of burnishing trees,
resting your gaze
in the emptiness between,
the light dances up
everywhere at once
and in a brilliant profusion of glyphs,
the hidden shape of the water
is stammered-out by the wind

— yet, with a certainty
you are not here to see.

still this light fills my heart,
        which now declines
                        to keen

What the Sea Offers Up
Claudia Van Gerven

Bundles of seaweed like the bodies
of fallen heroes. They are lifted up
offered to the shore wrapped in sea-swaddling
in the fecund rot of sea-graces.

Long kelp pods squirming up the shore
sperm indentured to the wish for life.

The constant weave of sands, sluicing
through water fingers, turned and braided
laced with grasses, with fronds, pocked
with shells, stones small as buttons.

Jelly-fish with their see-through bellies, stings
curled in perfect lavender circles.

The two dead gulls, lathed and lifted
in the lap of patient waters, beaks tucked under
splayed wings, flirting lovers or Spanish
dancers, feathered joints loosening,
small bones, small boats
moored in this vastness

Afloat in Paris

Dianalee Velie

> *There are days when solitude is a heady wine that intoxicates you with freedom.*
> — Collette

Afloat in Paris, I drift in my dream,
the Seine gently swaying le Autobus,
the bells praying the twelve-noon angelus
from Notre Dama's towers rising upstream.

Rewriting the Book of Love, self-esteem
won at great expense, I am a nimbus
afloat in Paris. I drift in my dream,
the Seine gently swaying le Autobus.

Single-mindedly catching a sunbeam,
surreal light surrounds my aloneness.
Content for the moment like Narcissus,
I am not as lonely as I may seem.
Afloat in Paris, I drift in my dream.

130

RIVER: A PILGRIMAGE TO WATER (EXCERPT)

REBECCA VINCENT

Avalon: Finally, I arrive at the river with my solo canoe, my favorite paddle, my spare in case my favorite gets away from me, my life jacket, my cooler, my backpack, everything I need. Finally, I leave behind my life on land, my duties as a parent, as a partner, my to do lists, bills, phones, cars, computers, I leave it all behind. I am finally here just for me, just for this river.

I come to this pristine river in Northwestern Wisconsin to leave even my self behind; to become the light-filled swirls of river water melting into the current, emptying of self and humanness. I come to the river to dream and gather stories; to share company with the moths, silt, and green fairies.

As I launch from the landing out into the smooth cool water, contentedness immediately envelops me. A kingfisher dives across the river, and I spy an immature green heron through the arrowhead plants on the left shore. Up ahead, a mama merganser and five babies follow the rippling current downstream. Black and green dragonflies land on my arm.

I settle into a slow, easy rhythm, no hurry, no agenda. Smooth black rocks that have lived in this river for thousands of years jut out of the water's surface creating a maze through the water. Groves of cedar trees line the banks on each side of the river. The water is alive, rich, and sparkling with green charms. It is dark and heavy in its pull toward the Great Lake. Pools of the river are sprinkled with foam. Long dark green plants anchored to the sandy river bottom sway in the current like mermaids' hair. Sunlight glistens on the river as if handfuls of shining diamonds were spilled upon its surface.

I'm paddling through the swirls of river water seeking stories, visions, words from the people under the water, from the rocks, from the mayflies.

This river, I remember sadly, is one of only nine percent of all streams and waterways in the lower forty-eight of the U.S. that is not dammed or manipulated in some way by humans. What great fortune for me to be in this living cathedral of green and open water. What grace to be swallowed by the ancient silence that lives here, the silence that is so rare in our world; to be breathed in by the trees and breathed out renewed, whole; to be washed in the cycles of life and butterfly wings. My medicine is to be swallowed whole by this.

Rivertime. Time to sweep through the cobwebs of city, of world, of engagements, problems, and to enter the dreamrealm; time to pull back the blinds and listen to the voices in the water. Time to disappear from humanness and to enter the songs of birds; to empty myself of me-ness and fill with what's larger than self, with the more-than-human. Time to drink from the Source that never dries and to enter the spells cast by the River; to become enchanted and lost, and to half-awaken from the spell washed anew.

I pull my canoe up to a small clearing where the roots of two old cedar trees have grown together to form an inviting bench right on the shore. I settle comfortably into the seat of cedars and drink tea. The long shadows of the tall trees above me join together and shimmer on the water. The shoreline is a tangle of smooth, sculpted old cedar trees whose gnarled roots and trunks entwine and support each other. Jade light filters through the branches above, casting a pearly-green translucence onto the water and shoreline. In turn, the flickering, sunlit river water is reflected onto the cedar roots lining the bank in silent shining pulses of light. In the pool of water before me, an amber-hued image of sky undulates with tall trees reflected in the river's flow. It is as if I am in a little chamber of mirrors cast with a pulsing, living mix of water, sunlight, flowing sky, and animate cedars; as if glistening strands of liquid sunlight are being splashed all across this little alcove of cedar roots and moving water.

I can imagine hours passing here in this liminal space between shadows and light, shore and stream, water and dream; hours, even seasons, years, decades, lost, like in the old stories, in the realm of fairy. European folktales describe how mortals can slip or be taken into the world of the fairies, a bewitching realm of enchantment where time passes differently than in the mortal world; upon returning home they sometimes find years have gone by in what seemed like minutes or days in fairyland.

The linear time of our modern, mechanical world has evaporated for me here on the riverbank, and I have become lost and calm in the long mesmerizing shadows and reflections of curving, dancing cedars on water. It is as if a wand of magic, or a hazel rod dipped in the waters of otherworld touched this stream and its shores, its tangles of branches lining its banks, and transfixed it into another realm, into dream and the place beyond time. It is as if the veils have been lifted, and I've slipped into the dreamspace of Avalon, the legendary Apple Island of Arthurian lore where supernatural beings were said to reside and where the earth willingly yielded fruit and grain with no labor required by people; a land of beauty and magic where old powers reign and where otherwise fatal wounds may be healed. Avalon was said to have been shrouded in mist which hid it from most mortal eyes and kept it inaccessible. On certain fortuitous occasions, though, the veil of mist would be lifted and lucky beings could slip by boat into Avalon.

Thirst: Could I be here, lost in Avalon, I ask myself, if this river were not one of the few which remains unshackled by people? Would I experience this sense of euphoria and rebirth paddling on the Ocoee, a river turned on and off each day by the Tennessee Valley Authority; a river dissected by dams and siphoned by pipes and tunnels. We as a species seem intent on touching and manipulating every last hidden corner of wild space. But what would I and people like me do to regain balance, breath, a sense of centeredness in this jangling, loud, and tumultuous world without natural places left alone by people; places not carved up and imprinted by the human hand?

Plans are being made for many of the remaining nine percent of U.S. streams and rivers that aren't already dammed and shaped by people. And water tables are dropping around the globe. Having discounted spirit in matter and water, we as a species have similarly lost awareness of water's physical limitations. On every continent of the Earth people are using water far more quickly than it can naturally be replenished. In some areas, to support large-scale industrial farming, we are drawing heavily on "fossil" reserves of water which have taken millennia to accumulate; waters which, if they regenerate at all, will take many thousands of years to do so. In just a blip of geological time we are heedlessly depleting the Earth's capital of water.

My worries about water follow me here onto the river, and although mostly I am lost in the bliss of being on this beautiful river, my Avalon, my thoughts bring me back now and again to anxieties about how we are living collectively on the Earth and our massive mismanagement of water. I think of one of the more widely publicized water depletion stories, the Aral Sea in Central Asia. Once the world's fourth largest lake, the Aral Sea lost eighty percent of its water after Soviet officials, in the 1960s, diverted two major rivers that fed it for a massive irrigation project to grow cotton in the desert. The amount of water loss from the Aral Sea is more than 1.5 times the volume of Lake Erie. And in Africa, Lake Chad, once clearly visible to astronauts in space, is now difficult for them to find. The lake has dwindled ninety-six percent in a span of forty years.

And then there's global warming. Our beautiful planet is melting, and we're the ones turning up the thermostat. Glaciers are melting, lakes and streams are evaporating, springs are going dry all around the Earth. In the Tibet-Qinghai Plateau of China where many of Asia's major rivers originate, 3000 of the 4000 lakes have evaporated in the past twenty years due to the warming of the Earth's climate. I think about what the loss of those thousands of lakes might mean to the people, birds, and other animals living near to them. I imagine the people who depend on rivers flowing from those lakes for water—for drinking, washing, and growing food—and I ponder how they would cope with the disappearance of those precious streams. I picture in my mind the dusty dry riverbeds and thirsty people. And I imagine what the loss of those lakes and rivers might mean to people emotionally and spiritually. I imagine how I would feel if this river I paddle through today were to disappear.

My paddle slips silently through the water. There is nothing here except me, this river, and my wandering thoughts about water. I consider how glaciers, which have existed since before the dawn of agriculture, are melting at an accelerating rate, threatening drinking and irrigation water supplies around the world from the Western United States to South America, Kenya, India, China, and many other parts of Asia. I see the towering mountains, always snowcapped, now dry. Around the Earth we risk calamities of unimaginable magnitude if global warming and glacial melting continue unabated.

Already, according to the World Conservation Union, one in seven people on the planet does not have enough clean water to drink. If current trends continue, by 2025 two-thirds of the world's population will be living with severe water deprivation. Along the US-Mexican border and, I'm told, in certain Alaskan villages, some families are raising their children on Coca-Cola because the cost for clean water is prohibitive.

flitting through trees, whole scenes of life as it has been lived the past three billion years; the stitches in the wool unraveling, slowly at first, but then ever faster until it's swept up in a frenzied whirl of motion and speed, enveloped in a blind and unalterable course of loss, disintegration, starvation, and death.

In the old days people gazed into clear basins of water hoping to see glimmers of the future. Watching this calm pool of river, I look in my mind and imagination for what our future might hold. The dream-water images pull me into ever-darker pools of possibility. . . .

Sand rushes over the Earth's surface, dust blows into dust . . . vast stretches of endlessly flowing sand . . . deserts advance . . .winds blow through dead trees . . . emptiness onto emptiness . . . just the sand now, blowing white in the sun, erasing our tracks as it plows across the dry lake's surface. . . this brokenness, broken shells, cracking, breaking underneath our bare feet as we walk along the stony desert sand and dry riverbed . . . waves of wreckage and debris crash and roll . . . we spin in chaos . . . dry thunder cracks . . . we're on dry land, desert-scorching red, bathed only in the dry yellow brightness of noon day delirium . . . dried up fields and hills blow in the wind.

A ripple of wind disturbs the water's smooth surface, and the dream images retreat from its mirrored surface. Then silence, stillness.

How do we reverse this flow, O River, O Ancient One? Give us a vision, I pray, a plan of action for the collective, a way to nourish and cherish once again the vast holy green garden and all its inhabitants. Pour your waters through our parched souls, O River; wake us up, I beg, and bring us back to life.

Naples, Florida

J. Weintraub

There's safety in this sameness
and strength, too, to help tame this
uncertain life that we lead. The histories
we tell our children, we carve in stone,
an epic poem of our pasts, our victories
and losses; words, deeds in monochrome.
Easier to remember that way and repeat
again and again, like the news
we watch every night, and the views
we hold dear, and the lies, and the waves on the beach . . .
the work to be done, days to be framed,
the same gardens to tend, the same lessons to teach,
for every attempt, venture, and gain,
one day to the next, always the same;
as if preserved in amber by the years,
archaic insects—until time
grabs us by the throat to remind
us we've grown old and weak and need to fear
the seasons, our new neighbors, the streets;
and so we convert winter retreats
into homes and equity into bonds
to bask in the Florida sun,
in the flow of interest that compounds
each day as the waves, one-by-one
from the gray gulf up the shell-encrusted shore
fold and unfold, like the insistent kiss
of the tides, wave after wave, they slither toward
us and recede with a slow, rolling hiss.

Early Morning Conversations, Baja

Anthony Russell White

Someone says there's a whale
out there with her calf.
The small shorebirds say,
I'm still hungry, let's look
over there for crabs.
The ocean says, Watch out!
I'll swallow you whole—
spit your bones across a thousand
beaches just like this one.
The slim shadows of the palms say,
stay with me, I'll lead you to darkness.
The rock says to the ocean,
won't you ever give up?
I won't, it answers.
Such utter chance, what arrives
on a wave and remains behind,
all that never makes it to shore,
or comes in and is buried.
The big-little whale child leaps over
its mother, lashes its tiny flukes, says,
this is all play anyway, says,
You're it.

THE RAFT AT LONGS PEAK INN
KARIN WISIOL

Bee-buzzing July before the lunch bell. By the pond
my father lazes on his bench, smears Nivea, scans
the *Rocky Mountain News*.

I pole off the island. Water slick between us mirrors
the Peak's gray razored face sliced crossways by Broadway,
scenery for the summer show.

Through binocs each year we watch confetti climbers
edge sideways to chimneys that funnel them up to the Notch.
We don't feel we're not breathing.

This year I know they tie together and why. The raft
tilts icewater onto my feet. This year I know
he keeps watch and why.

40

MISSING

MARIANNE WOLF

I promise you mothers of America, that your sons will not be involved in foreign wars. President Franklin D. Roosevelt spoke these words in radio broadcasts to the nation during his reelection campaign for a third term. It was the summer of 1940, and by the smiles the four of them flashed at the camera, wars anywhere were indeed foreign to them. Families across the country were staggering out from the Great Depression the same as my mother's family did in Joliet, Illinois.

This family photo is an image of a common life: the children of hard-working people, posed on a sunny, carefree summer day in what was the backyard of their home on Cora Street

My mother is the young girl, about nine years old with feet together, posture straight, and head focused forward at the camera. A big smile beams from her freckled face. With arms at her side, she is holding the hand of her younger sister, Charlotte, a tiny four-year-old. Behind her is her oldest brother, Joe, who is wearing his hat pushed back and cocked to the side, revealing a thick tousle of dark hair reminiscent of Sinatra's style. The young woman in the light-colored, knee-length dress is her twelve-year-old sister, Millie.

There is one sibling not pictured, a brother Al who is sixteen years old. I know from other images and stories from this era that he is a tall, slim, thoughtful young man with a profound voice. My mother does not remember who took this picture; she suspects there were others taken along with this one, so possibly Al is the photographer.

Whenever I look at this image of my mother with her siblings, certain facts strike me. To have a camera in their house back then would have been an exciting event, and certainly one where all the siblings would have been present. Al is missing.

Within the next three years Al will have graduated from Joliet Township High School and been drafted to serve his country in the Navy. His ship, the *USS Johnston*, will be torpedoed and he will be listed among the missing in action, lost in the Battle of Samar, part of the greatest naval battle in history. The fatalities from the *Johnston* destruction would grow to list 186 fighting American seamen.

My mother often told me the story of how her family scanned the newspapers daily waiting for news of her brother. She described in detail what a sad time it was in their home, how her mother cried nightly at the prospect of what had happened and for the uncertainty of what was yet to come. It was painful for my mother and her siblings to go about their normal routine when there was no longer anything normal about it.

After three days adrift, Al was found—shattered and clinging to a floating slice of ship wreckage in the center of the black sea. He saw his shipmates, buddies with real names and American faces and hard-working families left back home, disappear into the vastness of the water surrounding him. He was nineteen and had already witnessed more than any man should have to in a lifetime. Raw, battered, and struggling for life, he would be among the lucky ones rescued, though to this day I know no more about his horror than I did as a young girl growing up alongside Al's daughter, my cousin Carol. There is little detail available about the Battle of Samar, part of the larger Battle for Leyte Gulf during the fall of 1944.

Records report that Japanese surface gunfire sunk destroyers Hoel, Johnston and destroyer escort Samuel B. Roberts on October 25. Destroyer Heermann and destroyer escort Dennis were damaged. The *Johnston* would damage the heavy cruiser Kumano before being hit. But other than this short brief, historians did not speak about the *USS Johnston* and its crew any more than my uncle ever did.

My mother explained to me that when her brother came home he didn't say anything about his experience. No battle stories, no heroics, not about the sinking of his ship, or his rescue. Years later as a child, I have a memory of overhearing my aunts vaguely whispering about Al losing his best buddy when the ship went down, and how he didn't want to talk about it.

My mother's family is a miniature replica of American society in itself. Its importance lies in the fact that it continues to cement us together by providing us a past, a present and a future.

When I stare at that aged black-and-white photo of my mother and three of her siblings it is my mother, not the oldest, not even the second-oldest holding her younger sister's hand in the pose. At that brief moment, my mother seems to be the caretaker.

Ironically, as life would play out, it would be my mother and her brother, Al, who'd together become the "caretakers" out of this family of five children.

With childhood memories and family stories passed on over the years, my mother and her brother showed the most concern for each other, their siblings, their parents, and the family pets.

It could have been that on the very day my mother was born in 1931, her father received a pink slip from the EJ&E Railroad. She often told me learning the facts of the day she was born made her grow up understanding the strength of family. To my grandfather, it must have appeared that life had hit rock-bottom on what surely had to be a terrible day of disillusionment for him. With three children, a wife and in-laws living under one roof at the time, I can only imagine his tears of sadness and surprise opening the front door to the cries of his newborn baby girl.

Afflicted by scarlet fever as a child, my mother's illness grew her determination not to be left behind in grade school. Because of her own pain, she understood personal struggle at a young age. Maybe because my mother learned at the apron of her own mother the pain in the silence of her brother's wartime suffering, she understood what he had left unsaid.

Through my mother's eyes, I have learned she often recognizes the struggles and sacrifices in others when most people do not.

Like my mother, my Uncle Al understood the importance and complications of family.

I have wonderful and scary childhood memories of my Uncle Al. His deep, bellowing voice always seemed to let my cousin Carol and me know he meant business when our play-date escapades got a little too noisy. Neither of us ever wanted to be on the receiving end of a scolding from him.

There was a side of my uncle, though, that I always remember vividly. Carol and I enjoyed many sleepovers at their house. Her big bedroom was on the second floor, at the top of a long staircase. As a child, at night, with the lights out, it was sometimes frightening to me. Carol and I would begin to squabble over keeping the light on in that long staircase. Just enough I thought, so I wouldn't be scared. During many of those quarrels, Carol and I would hear the door at the bottom of the staircase squeak open. Immediately, we went silent. And then, just as soft and tenderly as he could, my uncle would announce, "Leave the light on."

Throughout my life I've often thought about him missing, adrift in the darkness of the sea. I close my eyes to imagine his thoughts and fears when it strikes me—a man who'd been lost at sea understood the importance in calming my childhood fear.

To this day, each night I leave a light on. I know not if it calms my fears or lights the memory of my uncle.

Remembering Harding Lake
Nancy Woods

You know that lake
that round, ripple-skinned lake
that bowl-bottomed lake
that's lined with grass?
Would you meet me there
to shed our personalities
at the shore
along with our skin color
parents and places of birth
to dip soul-naked
into the deep
and risk coming out
just human?

WILDERNESS

PAULA YUP

I am a brute beast
and a wondrous and gorgeous creature
foaming with life. Even my elbows glisten
brown with sweat as I press palm against palm.
A creature bound to the earth,
I chew to sustain my grace and wild eyes,
and praise mushrooms, the feel of the them.
I can stretch my fingers like bamboo shoots
to touch leftover birds fallen from cloudbursts.
My black mane, beneath a moon
half-hidden behind cloud tufts,
is magnificent at night.
My eyes glisten. I am an animal fierce with light,
blue-black still trees are sentries guarding me,
and the sweet smell of black sky is the blanket of my delight.
I stalk more stars, more songs,
and sweep into a platter lake, wet as any fish.

46

Lake Michigan

Peggy Zabicki

Do you get tired of me
coming to you only when I need something?
Taking your cool arms
I wrap them around
me
to soothe the harshness of my day.
I return just to smell you
and steal your treasures.
You will never leave me.
I know this.
You are strong enough to keep me with you,
but you always let me go.
I leave you sitting
alone
when I have what I need.
You give me pink sugar sunsets and gold coins
dancing in the moonlight.
I give you nothing but my tears and fantasies.

TALLGRASS WRITERS GUILD

TallGrass Writers Guild is open to all who write seriously at any level. The Guild supports members by providing performance and publication opportunities via its multi-page, quarterly newsletter, open mics, formal readings, annual anthologies, and the TallGrass Writers Guild Performance Ensemble programs. In affiliation with Outrider Press, TallGrass produces its annual "Black-and-White" anthologies, the results of international calls for themed contest entries. Cash prizes and certificates awarded result from the decisions of independent judges. The Guild is a rarity among arts organizations in that it has been and remains largely self-sufficient despite the challenges facing non-profit arts organizations. For more information on TallGrass Writers Guild membership and programs, call 219-322-7270 or toll-free at 1-866-510-6735. Email tallgrassguild@sbcglobal.net.

THE JUDGE

Diane ("Diva Di") Williams, author of *Performing Seals*, is a prize-winning poet and essayist who has a novel in progress. A graduate of Chicago's Columbia College, "Judge Diva" was awarded a literary fellowship that took her to Ireland for extensive study. She lives and writes in Chicago, and teaches at Kendall College.

THE EDITOR

Whitney Scott plays many roles in Chicago's literary scene. She is an author, editor, book designer and reviewer whose poetry, fiction and creative nonfiction have been published internationally, earning her listings in *Contemporary Authors* and *Directory of American Poets and Fiction Writers*. A member of the Society of Midland Authors, she performs her work at colleges, universities, arts festivals and literary venues throughout the Chicago area and has been featured as guest author in the Illinois Authors Series at Chicago's Harold Washington Library. Scott was awarded the 2009-10 Writer-in-Residence Award from Bensenville Public Library, judged the 2010 National Federation of Press Women writing competition, and regularly reviews books for the American Library Association's *Booklist* magazine.

Best wishes to Outrider Press
and
TallGrass Writers Guild

Maggie Reister Walters
CLU, ChFC, CLTC

522 E 86th Ave.
Merrillville, IN, 46410
219.756.3849
Fax: 219.756.4103
Cell: 219.308.0137

mareister@financialguide.com

To Order
Outrider Press Publications
effective January 1 2006, all prices include applicable taxes

_____ **Deep Waters–$21**   _____
    Rivers, lakes, naval warfare, emotional depths
_____ **A Bird in the Hand: Risk and Flight–$21**   _____
    Casinos, runaway teens, and birds, birds, birds
_____ **Seasons of Change– $21**   _____
    The natural world, technology, personal identity
_____ **Fearsome Fascinations–$21**   _____
    Bad boys, vamps, werewolves, forbidden fruit
_____ **Wild Things–Domestic and Otherwise**   _____
    bats, rivers, children running wild
_____ **A Walk Through My Garden–$21**   _____
    Crocuses, digital gardening, farms, flowerpots
_____ **Vacations: The Good, the Bad, and the Ugly–$20**   _____
    From stolen moments to Roman holidays
_____ **Falling in Love Again–$20**   _____
    Love the second time around
_____ **Family Gatherings–$20**   _____
    Weddings, wakes, holidays and more
_____ **Take Two–They're Small –$20**   _____
    Food, food, food
_____ **A Kiss is Still a Kiss–$19**   _____
    Romantic love
_____ **Earth Beneath, Sky Beyond–$19**   _____
    Nature and our planet
_____ **Feathers, Fins & Fur–$18**   _____
    Animals
_____ **Freedom's Just Another Word–$17**   _____
    What is freedom–its responsibilities and rewards?
_____ **Alternatives: Roads Less Travelled–$17**   _____
    Night shifts, new directions, the counter-culture
_____ **Prairie Hearts–$17**   _____
    Writings on the Heartland

Add s/h charges:
$3.95 for 1 book...$6.95 for 2 books...$2.50 each add'l   _____

                                              TOTAL

Outrider Press   _____
2036 N. Winds Drive
Dyer, IN 46311